MW01279926

DISCARD

10-97

# NO SAFE PLACE

**Mary-Rose MacColl** was born in Brisbane in 1961. She worked as a cadet journalist, nursing assistant and supervisor of boarders before moving into higher education as a photocopier operator. She now works as the vice-chancellor's executive officer at QUT. Mary-Rose holds degrees from QUT and the University of Queensland. *No safe place*, her first novel, was runner-up in the 1995 *Australian*/Vogel Literary Award.

# NO SAFE PLACE

## MARY-ROSE MacCOLL

ALLEN & UNWIN

GRACE A. DOW MEMORIAL LIBRARY
MIDLAND, MICHIGAN 48640

This novel is fiction. There is no Walters University and the characters are products of my imagination. The sexual misconduct case is not based on any case I know of in Australia or elsewhere and I made it up following research. Any similarity between something in the novel and any real person or institution is completely coincidental.

Copyright © Mary-Rose MacColl, 1996

All rights reserved. No part of this book may be reproduced or transmitted in any form or by any means, electronic or mechanical, including photocopying, recording or by any information storage and retrieval system, without prior permission in writing from the publisher.

Publication of this title was assisted by The Australia Council, the Federal Government's arts funding and advisory body.

Australia Council
for the Arts

First published in 1996 by
Allen & Unwin
9 Atchison Street
St Leonards NSW 2065
Australia
Phone: (61 2) 9901 4088
Fax: (61 2) 9906 2218
E-mail: frontdesk@allen-unwin.com.au
URL: http://www.allen.unwin.com.au

National Library of Australia
Cataloguing-in-Publication entry:

MacColl, Mary-Rose, 1961– .
    No safe place.

    ISBN 1 86448 174 9.

    I. Title.

A823.3

Set in 10/12 pt Palatino by DOCUPRO, Sydney
Printed by Australian Print Group, Maryborough, Victoria

10 9 8 7 6 5 4 3 2

# ACKNOWLEDGEMENTS

Thanks to the many people who helped me with this novel . . .
Jan McKemmish, Belinda Ogden, Jo Fleming and Sasha Marin
from the University of Queensland creative writing course for
suggestions about many drafts. QUT my employer for professional development leave to write and especially Dennis
Gibson for encouragement and good conversations about
writing. David Gardiner and Eddie Scuderi for wise counsel.
Bernadette Foley for fine editorial advice and a keen eye and
Sophie Cunningham and Annette Barlow from Allen & Unwin
for turning the manuscript into a novel.

# ONE

Rain stings my face as I walk to the car. I'm late but I take the beach road anyway. The windscreen fogs. My eyes keep closing. There's a bad taste in my mouth. Did I have pizza last night? Port Phillip Bay is slow and thick, sleepy white caps ease out of the grey-green. The road twists with the shoreline and has a dull sheen like pewter. My mother has a cabinet full of pewter.

The traffic backs up at St Kilda and the mouth in the face of Luna Park smiles at me like Liberace. I catch myself in the rearview mirror, make a face like the face of Luna Park, push a cassette into the player. Carnival music. Carnival music? An American voice. 'Let's travel with Burlesque!' More carnival music. It's my French language tape. 'Hello,' says my American French teacher. 'Or *bonjour* as we say in France!' I can tell he's smiling, I eject him.

It's after nine when I pull into the carpark. I've forgotten my umbrella. 'Hey Miss Lanois,' George is sitting in his cage at the entry. He pronounces my name *La-noise* like it's spelled instead of *Lanwah* like it's meant to sound. He's chewing something.

I zap the window. 'I'm late George.'

'I'll park her for you Miss, you go up.'

George has looked exactly the same for the five years I've worked at Walters University—uniform dark pants and light blue shirt, oiled black hair, dark parka, fur collar. I know I should say something to him about gender-neutral language.

1

Cars are not women and women are not cars. I know I should give him a copy of the university's policy on non-discriminatory conduct. But I don't. I leave the keys and make a mental note to buy him a bottle of something. I have no moral centre. It's the third time this month he's parked the car for me.

Walters University is seven buildings on the Yarra riverbank opposite the city centre of Melbourne. *The downtown university*, that was last year's advertising slogan. The centrepiece of the campus is the Business Tower, twelve stories of late-1980s black glass and granite shaved at an angle on top. Around the tower are three nineteenth-century redbrick buildings and the sandstone Walters House. They sit quietly as if they're waiting for something to happen. Terraced down the slope to the river are two new buildings: the Performing Arts Academy with its panels of orange and purple corrugated iron and glass. And the Chancellery Building where I work, quiet, off-white and austere.

Two men in dark suits and dark glasses are waiting at the lift and we stand side by side and stare at the indicator light. Once inside, I watch my reflection in the black plastic wall panels. I get a hazy version of myself like one of those black and white photographs where the contrast is so low the image is hard to pin down. I like this version of myself.

The Blues Brothers alight at the fourth floor where the Finance and Planning people work. I still don't know what they do even though they're part of my division now. I get out on the fifth floor and walk past our reception area where spotlights show off white walls and the black granite counter. It's all blond wood here like a magazine kitchen. The receptionist, who I call the receptionist's receptionist because some of the offices have receptionists as well, is like a bunch of flowers, salmon lips and purple scarf in an otherwise dull scene. It's quiet here in the soothe of air-conditioning and computing equipment.

All the interior walls on the fifth floor are glass, huge panels stuck together with black gunk, covered with vertical blinds. 'Natural light,' Bill Pozzi says. 'Natural light for the world of work.' It feels like a fishbowl with stripes. I walk

2

across the building through the open-plan interior that's like an ant farm, people moving around against the glass walls. I pass Bill Pozzi's office where the vertical blinds are closed. Along the corridor, towards the vice-chancellor's office, is my office where my secretary is looking for me. He smiles and tells me I have a nine o'clock.

'Hi John. Who?' I want to look as if I got out of bed hours ago. I use energy to smile and run my hand across my forehead. I'm sure my face is still creased with a sheet mark. Did I do my hair?

John is staring at me. His eyes are enlarged by Coke-bottle glasses. I'm sure he knows I just woke up. 'Gareth Ford from Student Counselling. He's waiting outside.'

'I forgot.' I didn't notice anyone as I came through. Gareth Ford. The name's vaguely familiar. I look towards John's computer screen at the week's diary full of appointments. 'What's all this? I thought we were going to keep this week clear for me to work on the quality submission.'

'We were. You put most of these in, not me.' I try to find an appointment he put in but I can't.

My room is large for me but the smallest of the three executive offices. There's a long blond desk with a drop-down keyboard computer return on the side. At the desk, there's a typist's chair on wheels with a worn blue upholstered seat. When I was made registrar last year, they bought me a leather executive chair, but it wasn't comfortable so I gave it back. Next to the desk is a cupboard and a bookcase. In the corner diagonally opposite, there's a coffee table with four cobalt low-back chairs, the kind of chairs you sink into and struggle out of. They match the now closed blue vertical blinds on the interior glass wall.

I throw my satchel into the cupboard and check my hair in the mirror inside the door. It's basically combed although it's so long now I should tie it back for work. I discover a large patch of foundation on the side of my face that's a different colour from the rest of me. No wonder John was staring. I wipe my cheek with the palm of my hand until the make-up blends in. My eyes are still puffy from sleep. I turn side on. I'm getting fatter. There are no angles where my chin should be.

My mother is standing at the river window looking back towards me. She's a tiny thing, that's what people say about her. She has long dark brown hair parted in the middle and tied up, her skin is white, her lips are thin and red and her chin is a statement of strength. I have her hair and skin. She's wearing a silky pink nightdress with a matching coat covered in green and crimson roses. She smells of those bags of dried flowers people put in their linen cupboards. She's talking softly, about Faith Cunningham. Faith Cunningham is the most popular girl in my class and the best at netball. Her hair goes green from swimming. Mummy says she matured too early. 'It's not good for girls, they get into trouble.'

'What sort of trouble?'

'Just trouble.'

I go to my desk, open a file, close it, move the phone to the left, straighten the blotter, close my eyes until my mother goes.

I walk out to the waiting area and see my appointment before he sees me. He's sitting forward in a straight chair, his back is curved, his elbows rest on his spread knees, his chin rests on his closed fists and he watches a spot on the carpet about six feet in front of him. I remember him from some meeting or other. He has a beard and glasses with round dark rims. He might be religious. I put out my hand.

'Gareth, Adele Lanois, I think we've met before.' I smile but he doesn't respond. 'Sorry I'm late, I was held up.'

He says hello in a soft warm voice. He stands up and shakes my hand, I get that electric snap of two dry bodies meeting, his hand is large and soft. He's taller than me by a whisper, maybe five ten. He looks at his watch. I think he's angry with me. He follows me through the security doors and back down the corridor to my office. I feel him looking at me critically. I pull at the front of my jacket which buckles at my hips. I tell him to sit down at the small table where John has left a plunger of coffee. I sit on the chair next to him, start on the coffee plunger which is difficult to push. He leans forward,

4

grabs my hand. 'I'll show you something.' I'm aware his hand's on top of mine and I don't move. I'm a moment shy of embarrassment when he lifts the plunger half an inch, I pull my hand away, he replunges, lifts, replunges. 'This makes it easier,' he says. I take over, he's right, it is easier. I pour coffee, sit back, we shift our chairs around, half face one another, towards the view.

I look at Gareth Ford properly for the first time. He seems friendly. Maybe he's not angry at me. I hate people being angry at me. He's wearing dark brown corduroy pants, a large cream jumper that hangs loosely with a white shirt underneath, no tie. He has wavy auburn hair in a nondescript cut and a reddish sandy beard. He's not handsome exactly but I feel comfortable about the look of him. I get an impression of carelessness.

'This is a great office,' he says, looking through the windows to the city. I notice fine gold hairs and dull freckles on his hands which rest on his thighs.

'Actually, I moved my desk into the corner because the view was so distracting,' I say.

'If I had this office, I'd never do anything.' He smiles for the first time. He looks boyish when he smiles, vulnerable around his eyes which I keep noticing. They're very blue.

'We have met before haven't we?' I say.

'You chaired the selection panel that appointed me.'

'That's right,' I say, not remembering. 'When was that?'

'Nearly three years ago.'

'With Max Neumann?' He nods yes. I remember now. We nearly gave the job to someone else, a woman, I got into trouble from the equity people for appointing him. I must have been acting registrar. Maybe it was when Tom McIntyre first got sick. Tom McIntyre was registrar before me. 'You came from Adelaide, didn't you, from Bass Uni? Weren't you an academic?' He says yes. 'Now I remember. We thought you were a real catch.'

'I was.' We both smile.

'You still in the same job?' He is. 'Counselling's a good department.' He agrees. 'I expect you'll be the stars in this year's quality review.' I smile. Quality reviews are a Federal Government initiative, each year they send a team of experts to rank universities, hand out money. This year, the topic is student support services.

'Walters—the university that values students,' he says. He looks at me above his spectacles.

'That's right.'

'A slogan based on the theory that if you say something often enough people will start to believe it.'

'You don't think we value students?'

'Do you?'

'Yes I do. Your department's a good example. You offer good services to students. You ask them what they think about what you do. You make changes. That's quality.'

'You're writing our submission aren't you?'

'Yes I am so unless you've got a great student service story to tell, I don't want to know.' I laugh, he doesn't, there's a pause that stretches. 'Only kidding. How can I help you?' I place my hands on the arms of my chair.

'You sound like a counsellor.' He looks from me to the desk to the window and back. I smile to appear reassuring. He pushes his glasses up his nose then pulls them back down, pauses so long I nearly say something, and finally speaks. 'I've had some trouble.' He looks towards the floor. For a moment I think he's going to cry. He breathes in and out through his nose.

'Go on,' I say, more to fill the space than anything else. I look over at my desk then at the fingers on my left hand, flick them against my thumb.

He places a hard black plastic case with aluminium trim and combination locks on his lap, opens it and takes out an envelope. 'I got this yesterday.' He hands me the envelope, I find some documents, catch a few phrases here and there, it's a statement of claim. 'I'm being sued by a client,' he says. 'A student here at Walters who says I seduced her.' He looks up at me, holds my gaze with eyes like Jesus until I look away.

'Have you talked to Max?' Max Neumann is his boss.

'He said to see you.'

6

I read the claim. 'This is pretty serious Gareth.' I have a real talent for stating the obvious. I pick up a glass paper-weight from the table and roll it around in my hand. He watches me. I watch him watching me. 'Just tell me every-thing you know and I'll read this later.'

'There's not much to tell. Jane Kidman was one of my clients, here at the university and then in private practice.' I look a question at him. 'I have a private practice from home. When students need more time than I can afford here at uni and they've got money, I suggest private therapy.' I motion him to pause, go over to my desk, find an A4 notepad, sit down again and tell him to go on. 'I saw Jane once or twice a week for eighteen months. Six months ago, I suggested she have a break. I felt she'd come as far as she could with me. I gave her the name of a psychiatrist I know who specialises in her sort of issues. I don't know if she took up that option. Then I got this.'

'That's it?'

'That's it.' He sits back in his chair with his hands on his knees.

I look at the claim again. 'Can you think of any reason why she'd make allegations like this?' I look at him, I look at his eyes. He looks back at me, says he doesn't know, says there's no question about it, he'd never do that, says he's devastated. I tell him I appreciate how he feels. I don't believe a word.

'I know what you're thinking,' he frowns, 'how this must look. I've counselled people who've made claims like this,' he gestures towards the paperwork. 'I didn't question for a minute they were telling the truth.' He smiles weakly but the edges of his mouth and his eyes don't mean it. For a moment, I feel sorry for him. I look out the window where light steamy rain blankets the world. He follows my eyes. I look at him directly again. 'Nobody believes the therapist,' he says. 'I know the more I tell you I'm innocent, the more you'll think I did it.' He pauses again, blinks a few times. 'I just can't believe this has happened to me.'

I assure him the university won't make assumptions about his guilt or otherwise. I point out he's innocent until proven guilty, tell him about professional indemnity. The university indemnifies its staff in carrying out their lawful duties. We'll protect him to the extent of the law if someone wrongfully accuses him, hurts him, damages him. I tell him he's insured against civil action as long as he's acted properly. I gloss over the part about acting properly. What's the point at this stage? We'll sort it out soon enough. I tell him we can't act for him, he should get a solicitor. I tell him I'll be back in touch when I know more. I stand up, let him know it's time to finish. I ask John to copy the documents for me.

As he's leaving he says, 'Max said you were an honest broker.' He grabs my hand. There's no electric snap this time. I look down. He lets go.

# TWO

I stand at the window and watch bland grey rain. Sexual misconduct. A staff member and a student. A psychotherapist and a client. A middle-aged man and a young woman. This is going to be ugly. It's going to be one of those cases you read about, one of those cases everybody loses. I feel as if it's been raining for months.

I go outside. 'What's next John?'

'Ten o'clock with the DVC, I told him you'd be late. You're scheduled for a demo of the Tower security system at lunchtime. And you've got a budget review at three.' He's holding a pencil with a chewed end near his mouth. I want to tell him to throw it away.

'Cancel the Tower and budget review. I want to spend today on that last appointment.'

'I thought you were working on the quality submission this week.'

'I am, but something's come up. Can you find out if we've been served with anything from Randall and Cross Solicitors. And I want a student file, Jane May Kidman, currently enrolled. I want the full file, not just her student record.'

Bill Pozzi is waiting with his door open. 'Sorry I'm late,' I say. 'I was held up at a meeting.'

'That's okay,' he says. But I know it isn't. Bill has a corner office that looks up and across the river, furnished in an expensive cherry coloured wood. There are gold handles on things that open and the desk is spotless except for a leather blotter holder, pen set and gold picture frame enclosing Bill's thin wife and their three fat sons. On the shelves behind the desk there are expensive books and a fussy oriental lamp. The off-white vertical blinds which cover the interior glass walls are closed. Bill sits on a leather lounge in one corner of the room, facing the view. He holds up his hand while he finishes writing something. The fat fingers of his other hand wrap around a fat expensive fountain pen. Behind him there's a dark green plant in a large white pot.

Professor Bill Pozzi is the deputy vice-chancellor, second in charge of Walters University and my boss. He used to be dean of Law so he knows my father. I think they worked together at some stage. He tells me to sit down, I walk over, wanting to be smaller, sink into the opposite end of the leather lounge. 'How're things?' he says.

I say things are fine. I smile and shake my hair around. 'Did you get the draft quality sub?'

'Thanks,' he says. 'I shot off a few comments this morning but I think it's very good. You work so fast on that sort of stuff.' Bill asks if Daniel has a copy. He has. 'The library comes up really well.' Bill runs the library so I guess he's pleased. 'And your division looks like we actually planned for quality.' He laughs.

'My division does plan for quality. There's some good work being done, especially in student services.'

'Who's in charge there now?'

'Max Neumann.'

'He's good.'

I agree. 'Bill, while we're on student services, can I talk to you about something?' I tell him about Gareth Ford and Jane Kidman.

'How old is she?' he says.

'Twenty now, eighteen when it started.'

He shakes his head. 'Have you talked to him?'

'He denies everything.'

'Of course.'

'We're joined in the suit.'

'Negligence?'

'Yeah, they say we failed to act on previous complaints.'

'Okay, pull the files, if there are previous complaints we'll find them. Then I guess we'll need to see Daniel, work out where to go from here.' He shakes his head. 'Poor kid.' We sit for a moment. His cheeks and chin are masked by what would be a beard in a minute if he didn't shave, it's like dirt on his face. I get an urge to yawn. 'Adele, is everything all right?'

'Yes Bill, why?' I'm still swallowing my yawn and my voice comes out all wrong, high pitched and scratchy.

'Haven't seen much of you lately.'

'I've been working from home to get the draft submission finished.' This is more or less true. I have been working on the quality submission, and I have been spending time at home. 'I've been really busy.'

'That's all?' Suddenly, I have no idea why, I feel as if I might cry. I swallow, nod yes. He smiles, sits forward, looks straight in front. 'How are you doing with the human resources plan?'

'It's in the pile,' I say. 'I'll get something to you this week.'

'Anything I can help with?'

'No it's fine, I just need time.'

He looks at me. I use energy to smile, look over at his desk. 'Okay.' He slaps his hands against his thighs.

I leave Bill with an assurance I'll get the HR plan to him next week. What else can I do? Even if I knew what was wrong with me, I wouldn't confide in Bill. When I first started at the university, I worked as the legal officer so my boss was the registrar, Tom McIntyre. I was in charge of liaison with the university's solicitors and Tom took me under his wing, we worked together on most things, I felt safe. But Bill's a lawyer, we had that in common, he thought I should know what to do, and he knows my father. I made mistakes. Once, I missed the meaning of a policy that wound us up in litigation. Bill was furious. Now Tom's gone and I'm the registrar so Bill's my boss.

I go back to my office. John looks up at me but says

nothing. Is he Bill Pozzi's source? Surely not. 'I want to work quietly for a while John.'

'Sure,' he says.

Sure? What does he mean? I close my door, power up my computer, I like its flat screen, the constant hum. I feel comfortable in front of a computer screen. Things seem simple. I take the documents Gareth Ford has given me and my notes from our meeting. I turn to the computer and think of typing something. But I don't type, I stare at the screen, fiddle with the mouse. Then I turn back to the desk, find a red pen and draw. I don't think about anything really, just let the morning roll over me. My mother turned up in the office again, Bill Pozzi thinks I'm an idiot and one of my staff is accused of sexual misconduct. I draw nothing much, not at first, lines, arrowheads, solid diamond shapes. Then I move on to another page and draw a small red face, it's Gareth Ford.

# THREE

I pull into a shopping complex off St Kilda Road where I
forget to buy milk. As I'm leaving I stop at a drivethrough
and buy a small sack of chips, a Coke and a children's burger.
I eat them on the way home and throw the rubbish under the
passenger seat.

The entry to my flat is through a gate in a high paling fence
at the end of a narrow laneway. Through the gate, along an
uneven cobbled path past Miss Bartlett's flat is my flat, two
thirds of a house really, Miss Bartlett's house. Miss Bartlett is
a thin medical secretary who lives in the other third. She
wears a clear plastic raincoat and a rainhat that concertinas
into a one-inch strip.

I hug a bag of groceries against the wall as I kick the front
door closed. My keys clatter on the sideboard. I hear the radio
in the kitchen and smell burned toast and something else
that's old and stale. I drop the groceries on the kitchen table
and go to my room to change. It's a mess. Single shoes adorn
the floor like a shoeshop. Clothes cover the unmade bed, the
dresser and oil heater. I undress, trying to remember which
piles are for dirties. I throw my jacket on the bed, take off my
shirt and bra, pull the wide legs of my trousers over my boots
and throw them after the jacket. I stand on the scales. A kilo
that wasn't there this morning.

I look in the mirror above my dresser, I'm still wearing my
boots and I look like something from some kinky fascist

movie. I turn on one side and bend down so I can see myself better. I've got a fat neck, I've even got a fat back, it drips down on each side as if the flesh has melted. My face is starting to become bland and featureless. I find a sweatshirt and tracksuit pants on the bed, go to the kitchen, switch on the light.

The kitchen in my flat is like an afterthought. There's only one bench, along the left wall as you walk in, topped with green marbled Laminex. At the end of the bench is my cyclic defrost refrigerator which needs defrosting three times more often than the brochure claimed. There's grey linoleum on the floor that might have been cream once, a stand alone gas stove and a wardrobe that functions as a pantry. The sink is on the wall opposite the door, on its own, the loneliest sink in the world. Above the sink there's a small window out to the back courtyard where Miss Bartlett scampers about with her two dogs hanging out and taking in washing when the weather changes.

I open the cyclic defrost, find some pizza, zap it in the microwave, put the kettle on the stove, sit down at the table and decide to call home. But I don't call straight away. I sit there at the table beside the phone, play with a bottle of antibiotics, emptying and refilling it with little maroon and mustard coloured pellets one by one, listening for the reassuring clink as each hits the bottom. I notice half a breadroll on a plate of leftover food that looks as if it's been nibbled by something other than me. Last week I found a hole in the bottom of a packet of crackers.

The kettle whistles and whistles before I switch it off. When I finally dial the number, I'm not ready when he answers. I pause too long. 'Hi Daddy it's me.'

He clears his throat noisily. 'Adele.' He sounds as if his voice comes from a long way away.

I ask how he is. He's sick. 'I think I'm coming down with the flu. Sore throat. I went out to the garden today when the rain cleared but I didn't feel like doing much.'

'That's no good,' I say. 'Been to the doctor?' He never goes to the doctor.

'See how I feel tomorrow.'

I ask after Mummy. She's fine. He asks about work. I tell him I got a pay rise which is a lie but I can't help myself. 'About time,' he says. 'But you'd still be better off in practice.'

'I heard on the news there was an accident down your way last night,' I say.

'Anglesea. Tourists.' He says tourists as if it explains everything.

I say that's awful. 'Was anyone killed?'

He doesn't know. 'They shouldn't take buses down here.' There's a pause. 'You coming home this weekend?'

'Yep, Friday night if that's okay.'

'Your mother will be pleased.'

I go out to the sitting room that adjoins my bedroom, light the gas heater, switch on the television, curl up in a satellite-dish chair, drink a glass of wine or two. Television shows come and go, something about a doctor who operated on people's backs and made them worse, they're suing him but nothing's proven. I eat some sundried tomatoes I find in the cyclic defrost, the pizza from the microwave. Later I have a bowl of cereal without milk. When I wake up it's morning and I've moved from the sitting room to my bed.

# FOUR

I sit at one end of a couch with the Gareth Ford file and stare at the red pen sketch I did of him after our meeting. It's not very good. He looks angry. He looks like my father who's sitting next to me, grey cardigan and white shirt from work, no tie. 'Don't you get it?' he says. 'It's not that difficult.' Flushed, frowning. Helping me with maths. Frustrated, hunched over because there's not enough room on the chair at the white desk in my bedroom. I feel so tired. 'Let's try another way.' He looks at me, mouth set tight, eyes moving from me to a point just beyond me, to the right and above my head. He sighs. I think I should speak but I don't know what to say. Silence. 'Adele.' I look up and see Jef Blackwell.

Jef Blackwell from Forest and Ryan is what Daddy would call slick. His hair is black with a blow-wave that doesn't move for anything. His suit looks as if it's part of his body. He has the most perfect hands and fingers I've ever seen. He lifts his heels and bows slightly when he greets me. He's clever, important, a partner and our lawyer.

I look to where Daddy was sitting but he's gone. I close the file, stand up. 'Did you get the papers?'

'Nasty case.' He smiles as if this is good news. I guess it is for him.

Bill Pozzi joins us, he's wearing a double-breasted suit but the coat's too long and it makes him look smaller and rounder than he is, especially standing with Jef and me who are both at least a head taller than him. 'Bill,' I say. 'You know Jef. We're seeing the VC.' We wait for a few moments, I think Bill's uncomfortable, he rocks from his heels to the balls of his feet. I'm uncomfortable too, I don't know why he's hanging around. We're rescued by the vice-chancellor who emerges from his office, takes two large steps to reach us, shakes my hand, smiles warmly as if he hasn't seen me in months, shakes the other hands, smiles some more. 'Come in,' he says to Jef and me. 'You coming into this Bill?'

Professor Daniel Reed looks more like a film star than a vice-chancellor, tall with a strong jaw and large white teeth. His hair is over his ears and collar. He jogs. He wears expensive suits with polished cotton shirts, talks slowly but not thoughtfully. He gestures with his hands which are long and feminine. Under stress he runs them through his wavy hair, holds his head in them and sometimes sits on them. His office is flat shiny surfaces, five uncomfortable chairs around a glass-topped table and a large blue vase on the desk. The lighting is soft and impractical.

I sit down and place the Gareth Ford file on the glass-topped table, squaring off two corners with my thumbs and index fingers. John, my secretary, has labelled the file *strictly confidential*. I place the university Act and statutes on top. I put my pen on the table to the right of the pile, sit back and fold my arms. I used to watch Tom McIntyre do this, he seemed so certain, so solid, I always felt so confident in him. I miss him most in meetings like this, cases where we'd work together.

We make small talk about the cricket which I don't follow, Bill and Daniel laugh loudly about something, I smile, pretend to get it. I shift in my seat, cross my legs, join my hands over my stomach. I'm wearing blue pants that feel tighter than last time I wore them, a white silk shirt that I haven't tucked in and a blue and green checked jacket. I notice myself in the mirror panel behind Daniel. I look unplanned. The coffee rattles in. The door closes.

Daniel has taken over his chair, he sits all over it, his right leg swinging over an arm, his left elbow resting on the other arm, his head resting on his left hand. 'Looks like we've got a problem,' he says.

'We sure have,' I say. I tell him Jane Kidman is suing the university and Gareth Ford. 'She's also filing complaints with the Victorian Psychologists' Registration Board and with the university under the staff misconduct by-law.'

'What does that mean?' Daniel says.

'She's covering the bases,' I say. 'The courts, his employer, his professional body. It's what I'd have advised her to do if I was her lawyer.' Bill grunts agreement. Jef looks at the fingers on his left hand.

'What's her story?' Daniel says.

'She was depressed, she went to see Ford, here at the university, then in his private practice. She says he had sex with her, breached his duty of care and she's damaged by the experience.'

Daniel is sitting on his hands. 'What do you think?' He looks at me.

'We'll have to investigate it as misconduct. Doesn't look good.'

Daniel nods. 'Okay, so what if we find him guilty?'

'I guess we do our best to minimise damages,' I say.

Jef Blackwell sits forward in his chair. 'Vice-chancellor, it's quite possible you could find him guilty of misconduct and still fight the legal case.' Daniel asks how. 'The claim against us is negligence,' Jef's voice just kind of rolls out of him. 'They have to establish two things. One, he initiated a sexual relationship.' He counts on his fingers as if we'll lose track otherwise. 'Two, we were negligent, we knew he might do something like this, we could have prevented it.' Daniel looks confused.

'What Jef's saying is that even if he's guilty of sexual misconduct, we'll only be liable if we were negligent,' I say.

Daniel smiles, rubs his chin, gulps coffee. 'What if we find him not guilty?'

I start to reply but Jef cuts in. 'That's easy. We proceed on the basis that Mr Ford hasn't acted improperly and that the university hasn't been negligent.'

'We can't know about something that doesn't exist,' Daniel says.

'Exactly,' Jef says.

Daniel takes a big breath in and blows out. 'From our point of view, we'd be better off if he's innocent.' He smiles.

'You'll find him as you find him.' Jef returns Daniel's smile, it disappears quickly. 'Whatever happens, the outcome will be substantial if the case goes against us.'

'Ballpark, what are we talking about?' Daniel says.

'A case like this, your responsibility for your staff, several hundred thousand dollars wouldn't be out of the ballpark.'

'Fuck, that's a floor on a building,' Daniel says.

'Quite,' says Jef.

Daniel leans forward, clasps his hands in front of himself. 'Sex is a big thing in counselling,' he says. His original discipline is psychology. 'When I was a head of department, we ran a counselling centre as a teaching clinic. Staff got involved with students now and then, it happened, it wasn't a big deal. In fact, that's how I met my wife.' He smiles. I didn't know this, I don't know if Bill did. Daniel's from the US and he's only been in the university a few years. 'But things are different now.' He pauses, looks past me and out the window, looks back at me, shaking his head. 'I'm thinking about the quality review, student support services, we've got to keep this out of the press.' He covers his forehead with his hand. 'The campaign!'

This year, Daniel wanted to stress the university as a service provider. We've been running a series of ads in the papers, radio and television. Instead of *The downtown university* we're *The university that values students*. I don't like the ads much, I think they're pitched at the wrong level. But I can see the irony. The press will have a field day with *The university that values students* when they hear about Gareth Ford.

'We can always talk with the other side about settlement,' Jef says.

'Good idea, see what they want,' Daniel says.

'I'd like to read the file first,' Bill says. We all look at him. 'And while I agree with Jef that in a strictly legal sense Ford could be guilty of misconduct without us being negligent, I think it's a pretty poor argument. If one of our staff has taken advantage of a student, we need to take responsibility. Obviously we have to investigate properly and see what we find. Dan, I'd be more than happy to head this up.'

'Is Jane Keating still enrolled?' Daniel says.

'Kidman. I've got her file here,' I say.

'What's she like?' he says.

'Good student, she'll graduate this year. Arts Journalism.'

'Great. Another outstanding Walters graduate with a grudge and a career in television. Anything else?'

'She made a complaint about another student a couple of years ago. The equity section's got the records.'

'Follow it up.' Daniel sits back in his chair, looks out the window, sits forward again, asks about the investigation. I tell him we have to set up a misconduct committee, I expect he'll appoint Bill. 'I'd like you to lead the investigation Adele,' he says.

'Sure,' I say. I can feel Bill next to me, pulling at my eyes. I don't look.

'How about Kit Jackson as well?' Kit Jackson is the equity director. I don't know her all that well. She's one of Daniel's new appointments. I nod agreement. I can't believe Daniel has missed Bill's offer to head the investigation. I feel uncomfortable, unsure about whether to say anything, wishing I were somewhere else.

'So, Bill's going to read the papers, make sure we're on the right track. Adele, you're going to set up your committee, investigate with Kit, come back to me before we go to university council. Jef, you're going to see what you can find out about a settlement in the court case.' Everyone is nodding. 'Can I get a copy of all the papers?'

'I'll get them to you today,' I say. 'Who'll handle media inquiries?'

'I will,' Daniel says. 'And I'll refer them to you if there's detail Bill.'

Bill walks out of the office without waiting for me.

# FIVE

'We're talking about a girl who was eighteen when this happened.' Kit Jackson, the university equity director and my co-investigator, has dark hair gone grey all over and white skin with faded pink cheeks. She wears black pants and a black sweater with a black jacket. I like looking at her. 'A girl who's had the courage to speak up. She's the one who'll suffer out of this, not him, no matter what they do to him.'

Kit's angry with me. She wants to take Gareth Ford outside and shoot him. 'I'd just like us to think about a structure for our investigation,' I say. 'Seems to me we have to answer two questions. For one of our counsellors, is sexual involvement with a student outside the university misconduct within the meaning of our by-law? And did Gareth Ford have a sexual relationship with Jane Kidman?'

'Yes and yes if you want my view.'

'That's interesting, but I wouldn't jump to conclusions about either question. Number one, the by-law's specific about what's misconduct and it doesn't mention sexual relationships. Number two, all we've got are unproven allegations, one person's word against another's.'

Kit gets up and walks around the room. She says no one makes sexual harassment complaints lightly, she says she understands my position but she's been around a long time, seen a lot of cases. 'They're all the same,' she says. 'People say the woman is lying. People say she made it up. But women never make it up. Why would you go through something like this unless you felt aggrieved?'

'I appreciate all that and frankly, just between you and me, I probably agree with you,' I say. 'All I'm suggesting is that we do our job, conduct the investigation fairly and objectively.' She tells me of course she's objective, asks wherever did I get the impression she'd formed a view, smiles.

She walks back over and sits down. I tell her I want to convene the first meeting of the committee next week, I want to wrap the whole thing up in a fortnight. I tell her I want to talk to Jane Kidman, Gareth Ford, his colleagues, his supervisor, other students he's counselled. I tell her she'll need to read the paperwork as soon as she can. I ask her to block out two days in her diary.

She says it's all fine except the part about Jane Kidman. 'She may not want to be interviewed.'

'I'll give her the option to talk to you and me rather than the full committee. If she refuses, we'll give her a list of questions through her solicitor.'

Kit says we must get together some time. 'There's a group of women from around the university, we meet at my place every couple of months, very informal, just to chat.'

I've heard of Kit's group, Daniel calls them the ginger girls. They want change, more access to senior jobs, more special schemes. I can't align myself with a group like that. 'I'm so busy in this job I don't get time for anything. But I'd love to come some time.' She says she'll call me.

I ask Kit about Jane Kidman's earlier complaint. 'Sexual harassment complaints are confidential,' she says. 'But it wasn't anything like this case.' She's looking at me. I ask her what it was like. 'A tutorial group complained about a student. Language and behaviour. Nothing like this.'

# SIX

My parents live an hour south-west of Melbourne along the Great Ocean Road at Fairhaven. When I was a little girl I thought I could see Tasmania from the back verandah of their house through binoculars that smelled of leather and cold metal. Tonight I feel a snap of cold when I open the car door so I grab my bag from the back seat and go inside quickly. I find Mummy in the kitchen. 'Hello darling, I'm so glad you decided to come.'

I hadn't said anything about not coming. Can she read my thoughts? We hug as Daddy emerges from the lounge, I'm still hanging on to my bag. He doesn't hug me anymore but he doesn't shake my hand either. He touches my shoulder and backs away. 'How's the law?' he says.

Five years ago I ended my short career as a practising solicitor when I walked out of a staff meeting and told my boss at Markham and Steiner I wouldn't be back. I called Tom McIntyre, Walters was one of my clients in those days, he said he was glad I rang, they were just about to advertise for an in-house legal officer, someone to liaise with their solicitors. Daddy was furious. Not because I left, he said, but because I left so suddenly. He said I never think about things. He said I've got no brains. Now he acts as if I never left.

'Actually I am involved in a case at the moment,' I say. 'Sexual misconduct.' He says we'll talk later, disappears out to the back door.

My mother produces a cup of tea and a chocolate biscuit. I say I'm trying to cut down on sweets, she says it's my favourite. I eat the biscuit. I take my bag up to my room, it looks as if I still sleep there every night, pink quilt and soft toys on the bed, white dresser with curly brass handles on the drawers, matching wardrobe with pretend shutter doors, white desk. On the door, there's a plaque with a neat black *Adele* on it that Daddy made when I learned to write my name. I open the apricot curtains, stand near the window-glass and stare into the cold blackness. Five years on and my father still pretends I'm a lawyer. The thing is, until I left the firm, I didn't realise how much I hated practising law, detailed forms and agreements that didn't seem to say anything or help anyone. I couldn't see the point. It was one of those impulsive decisions I've never regretted.

My mother calls up the stairs to me to please set the table when I'm ready. I go downstairs to the dining room which smells of a wood polish that will always remind me of boarding school. I take out cutlery, carefully place knives, forks and spoons on the table, things like this matter to my mother. It's dark in here even with the lights on, chunky wooden furniture, heavy drapes. When I was little, four or five, I used two cushions on a chair so I could reach my meal. I sit down. 'Adele, I've told you a thousand times to be careful at the table,' my father's hair is sticking to his forehead. 'For God's sake, look at me when I'm talking to you.' I watch milk crawl thickly towards the table edge.

'Alain, she didn't mean to spill it.' My mother's voice bruised and thin like the air in the room.

'You should have made her clean it up herself. I don't want a daughter I can't take anywhere because she's too clumsy. I think she does it to get me angry. Don't you? Don't you!' I close my eyes.

My father was large then and now I'm taller than him. When he works on the house in a singlet and overalls, I can see old muscles like tumours along his arms. He used to be powerful and smell of strong cigarettes. Now he has white hair and smells of talcum powder.

I change my mind about the table settings, put two knives and a fork at angles so they look less planned. Back in the kitchen Daddy's peering into the oven. 'What's for dinner?' I say.

'Lamb,' he says. He won't let my mother roast meats. He says she overcooks them.

'I thought I might go down to the water tomorrow.'

'That's a lovely idea,' Mummy says. 'Daddy might go with you.' She looks over to him but he doesn't respond. I stand there for a while watching them, he fusses over the roast, she chops, they seem so self-contained that I feel like an extra, relieved at the knock on the front door.

Uncle Jack and Auntie Clare hug me together at the doorstep. Uncle Jack says, 'I'm great sweetie, just great,' when I ask. He has a Scottish accent and his Rs crash in his throat.

Uncle Jack and Auntie Clare have lived next door to us for as long as I can remember. Jack's the architect who designed our house. He has a pink face with curly slate coloured hair. Auntie Clare has light blue eyes and lots of teeth. She's wearing a polo-neck jumper and her large breasts are like exclamation marks.

There's a fire going in the lounge, it makes orange and red lights in the doors of my mother's pewter cabinet. We get drinks and sit down on the new couch that goes around a corner. Daddy opens wine, then follows Mummy back to the kitchen. We talk about the house, Uncle Jack's extending his again, we talk about the neighbourhood, changes. 'What's happening in the real world?' Uncle Jack says.

'You asking me?' I say.

Daddy walks back in. 'Tell us about this case.'

'Daddy.' I look at him.

'Don't be silly. It's just Jack and Clare. Who are they going to tell?'

He always does something like this. 'You'll probably hear about it soon enough.' I tell them briefly about the case, no names of course.

'Where are you with it?' Daddy says. Jack and Clare look at each other and over to me, smiling.

'The vice-chancellor has asked me to lead the investigation.'

'Did you bring your notes home?'

'No.'

He scowls. 'What's your defence?'

'I haven't read all the material yet.'

'Want me to give Gordon Earle a call?' Mr Earle was one of Daddy's partners.

'We're getting advice.'

'Not from Forest and Ryan.'

'They're our solicitors.'

He grunts.

'Do you think he's guilty?' Uncle Jack says.

I say, 'That's a good question . . .' Daddy interrupts.

'Doesn't matter, it's whether you can prove it.'

'I'd be pretty worried if he did it and got off.'

'I'd say there's a good chance that's where you'll end up. He's innocent until proven Adele. Case like this, I don't like your chances of proving.' I tell him the university's by-laws are not as black and white as the criminal code, there's room for judgement. 'What if he didn't do it? What if she's lying and you people find him guilty, not because you've found proof, but because you just feel like he did it? Justice strives for truth based on evidence, facts, not feelings.'

'Was the student underaged?' Auntie Clare says.

'She was eighteen,' I say.

'So what's the problem?'

'Well Clare,' Daddy smiles, shows grey and gold teeth. 'If I engage Jack to design a house and instead he goes on a holiday, he's breached his ethics. It's the same thing. I engage you as a personal counsellor. Instead, you start a sexual relationship with me. You have a duty of care to me that you've breached.' He's setting up for a story when Uncle Jack cuts in.

'What if you engage me to design a house and I have sex with you?' We laugh and move to the dining room, Mummy serves, Daddy walks around the table as he pours wine. 'There was a case in Tasmania where they dismissed a professor who seduced a student. Same thing, her word against his, but no one believed him.'

'Someone mentioned it at work,' I say. 'What happened?'

He sits down. 'She claimed he seduced her. There wasn't much evidence, a diary, a letter she wrote him, one or two witnesses who might have seen them together. He denied it. The academic staff union was behind him because they saw it as interference with academic freedom for the university to dismiss a tenured professor. It went to the Supreme Court, I think it was Justice Green who said a university professor is liable to be dismissed for misconduct like any other servant and misconduct includes seducing a student.'

'The counsellor's not a professor,' I say.

'And you say the alleged misconduct was in his private practice, not at the university.' He smiles. 'I've got an idea. Even if you prove he did it, you might not be able to find him guilty of misconduct in the university. Because he didn't do it in the university.'

'I've thought about that.' Following my meeting with Kit Jackson, I went over the by-law. 'Misconduct includes any act or omission that damages the university. I reckon that includes his private practice since he's a professional psychologist who's an officer of the university.'

'Perhaps,' he says. 'Anyway, if she proves it, he'll be deregistered. You can sack him because he won't be qualified to do his job.'

'Maybe he didn't do it.' Having read the claim, I don't think this is likely but I can't help myself.

'What makes you think that?'

'What makes you think he did?'

'I didn't say I thought he did. You'd have to find a plausible reason why she'd pursue a false claim.'

'Money?'

'Maybe. I'll have to read the material. Bring it home next time and we'll have a proper discussion.'

We all agree the lamb is perfect with the claret Daddy's picked from the cellar. My father's family is from France and when his mother died the four boys wound up the family company. He was their youngest child and for some reason he inherited the wine cellar. We drink well.

When I wake up it's early, my head is aching and I'm aware of my eyes. I hear a tap running upstairs as I close the front door so I hurry to the car. It's cold on the beach and the sea sneaks around the shore as if it's got something to hide. I see a fisherman in thigh-length black boots and a yellow sprayjacket standing knee-deep in water. I imagine him being sucked down into the water by some monster that smells like oysters.

Jane Kidman's claim. Dates, times, thirteen separate sexual incidents, nine with intercourse and four with oral sex. She describes the seduction, how much she trusted him, what they wore, what he did, when he did it, how she felt. No witnesses. Always in his office. Hazy on consent. He denies it. Says he'd never do a thing like that. Daddy says he's innocent until proven guilty. Maybe he is. But he's guilty, Kit Jackson's right. You only have to read Jane Kidman's claim to know he did what she said. Maybe I can't prove it, maybe we'll never prove it, but I know for sure Gareth Ford had sex with Jane Kidman just like she says.

# SEVEN

On the way home I stop at the port at Geelong and watch men like ants crawling round huge ships to load or unload containers. It seems so fruitless. In Melbourne, I go to my room, clear clothes off the bed and crawl in. Half asleep in the warm dark, I'm in the large strong arms of Uncle Jack, flying up over his head, 'Here's my princess.' Down and up again, I lose my stomach, down, up, down, up. His face buried in my torso, blowing raspberries on my bare belly. 'Careful Jack, don't get her excited.' I'm upside down, my mother's eyes are at the wrong end of her face, her frown like a smile. Then it's morning.

And Gareth Ford is sitting outside the vice-chancellor's office staring at his hands. He doesn't see me straight away. I stop and watch him, think about how to avoid him. Then he sees me, smiles weakly and starts to get up. I acknowledge him as briefly and sternly as I can and walk past him into Daniel's office.

'Mr Ford, I'm Daniel Reed,' Daniel doesn't offer a hand. 'I think you know the registrar.' Daniel's good at staff discipline. He's put on his suitcoat. He tells Gareth to sit down, he sits opposite Gareth, motions me to sit with him. But for some reason I don't. I sit where I'm standing which is next to Gareth. Daniel sits back in his chair, crosses his legs. 'I understand you've already spoken with Ms Lanois about this matter and I won't waste your time and mine. We've received a complaint from one of our students that you became sexually involved with her.' Gareth nods. Daniel pauses, looks at Gareth. 'I'd regard behaviour like that from one of my staff as grossly unprofessional.'

'I'd never do something like that.' Gareth bumps my leg with his right knee as he speaks, looks at me and moves his leg away, I can still feel the warmth of him. 'You must understand that Professor Reed.' He looks down at the floor between his legs then at his hands which are clasped in front of him. He's wearing a suit, his lawyer must have suggested it. It's dark blue, looks as if he hasn't worn it for about a hundred years. He's tried to comb his hair, he's used gel or something. His shirt looks less than ironed. He's red around the eyes, hunched in the shoulders. He looks mentally disturbed.

'We want to find out the truth.' Daniel flashes a smile that disappears quickly. 'That's in everybody's interest.' He hands Gareth a signed letter that tells him he has fourteen days to respond in writing to the allegations.

'I can assure you these allegations are false,' Gareth says after he reads the letter. He looks at Daniel. 'Jane Kidman is very disturbed. She has serious problems, a history of child abuse. Really she needed professional psychiatric care.'

'Are you saying she made this up?' I say.

'Not exactly, I'm just not all that surprised.' Daniel and I look at each other, I raise an eyebrow. 'It's a special relationship, therapy,' Gareth says. 'Some clients, like Jane, become enraged, at the world really but they point it at their therapist. False allegations of sexualisation are quite common.'

Daniel uncrosses his legs and sits forward. 'We realise that,' he says. 'I'm a psychologist myself you know, so I know what you're talking about. And you'll have an opportunity to be heard on this. But these are serious allegations.' He stands up, walks over to the window. 'Gareth, I think for the moment it would be a good idea for you not to be at work.'

'What do you mean?'

'I've accepted a recommendation from the registrar that you be suspended from duty until further notice.' He looks at Gareth. 'You're in a vulnerable position. Maybe other allegations will be made, maybe falsely.'

'I thought I'd go on working,' Gareth says. 'It's like saying I did what she said I did.'

'No it's not. It's a case of protecting your interests and those of the university. We'll continue to pay you.'

'When I talked to Adele, she said the university would stand by me. I've been wrongly accused. Now you're saying I shouldn't come to work. I didn't do anything.'

'I appreciate your position Gareth,' Daniel looks at him. 'But I've got to think about everyone involved in this. This is to protect you as much as anyone else.'

I can't believe how easily Gareth accepts Daniel's offer. 'If you think it's best, I'll go along,' he says. 'But not by choice. I'm doing this to help the university. I want you to remember that.'

'I will,' Daniel says.

Gareth takes in a large breath, blows out through a small round mouth, swallows. I walk out with him, tell him I'll be in touch about the date of the misconduct committee meeting. We're outside the office in the foyer and he says, 'Adele, this isn't fair.'

'I'm sorry, we're in a difficult position.'

He looks at me, I want to go back into Daniel's office but his eyes won't let me turn around. 'Looks like I read you wrong, doesn't it?' He walks away. I think he's angry at me. I hate people being angry at me. I stand there for a moment before I turn around. The receptionist is looking over at me, smiling, as if I'm about to cry and she wants to cheer me up.

'What do you think?' I say.

'Sophisticated,' Daniel says. I look at him. 'Smart enough to look stupid.' He pauses for a moment. 'What do you think?'

'I wouldn't have said sophisticated. Actually, I thought he was a bit naive. He took the suspension pretty easily.'

'He didn't have much choice.'

'I guess not.' I ask if Daniel's read the complaint. He hasn't yet. 'There's a lot of detail, stuff that would be very difficult to fabricate. I can't believe she kept seeing him, but I'm almost

31

sure he did it.' Daniel nods, doesn't say anything. 'I'm getting going on the investigation. I think Bill would like to be involved.'

'I'm sure he would,' Daniel says.

'I think he might have wanted to head the investigation.'

'That's my decision, not his. I want you to head this investigation because I think you'll do a good job. Nothing against Bill, but he tends to side with students in these things. And we need to be fair and objective on this, not take sides.'

'I talked to Max Neumann,' I say. Daniel knows Max, I think he likes him. 'Gareth's boss. He says Gareth works well with students, fits into the department, staff really like him. Max asked me to talk to them, reassure them that we'll look into it thoroughly. They're pretty upset about it.'

'What does Max think?'

'He believes Ford. He says you can pick them.'

'O yeah,' Daniel says. 'Don't tell me, it's in their eyes.'

# EIGHT

I leave for work early and catch a cab to a club in the city for breakfast with a women's network. Two hundred of us sit in tables of ten listening to a business executive with a thin face and blonde hair like Barbie telling us about success and motivation. She's wired for sound and visuals, microphone pinned to her chest, computer-generated overhead slides with graphs where all the lines go up to the right. I look around the tables and notice that successful women wear red clothes, their hair is neither long nor short, they talk like men. I don't feel at home here.

Back at work, I'm looking for clues. 'We've searched back five years.' The records manager, Helen Yates, wears jeans, loose dull shirts and glasses that are nearly as large as her head. Her voice sounds forced, as if she doesn't want to be loud. She pronounces words in an exact way. 'There are a couple of letters about another Gareth Ford, a student who was in the Commonwealth Games,' she says. 'But there's nothing on the Gareth Ford on staff. It might help if you told me what we're looking for.' She grabs at her chest as if there's something there she needs to erase.

I haven't told her about the allegations. 'I can't give you details Helen. I'm just looking for external correspondence that refers to Gareth Ford.' I ask for the file that deals with complaints against staff. It's two large boxes, more than a dozen folders. I sit down in the reading room flicking quickly page by page through each folder. There's nothing. Why is

Jane Kidman saying we received complaints about Gareth Ford?

After lunch, Daniel, Bill and I meet the staff industrial unions. Five staff representatives sit opposite us at the small table in the conference room on the fifth floor. They tell us Gareth Ford's lawyer has been in touch with them, told them the full story, the academics support the general staff. On the wall behind them are three pieces from the university's art collection, part of a set called *Lived life*, in deep pink frames. There's a peg, an empty bean tin, a pair of underpants. I like looking at them, I like their unity. The air in the room is thin.

One of the union reps, a hairless lab technician from Health named Harry Gutterl, says, 'You suspended him without cause.' He has one of those finger-in-the-chest don't-mess-with-me voices and small eyes. His hairlessness suits his neck which is very thick.

'Not without cause,' Daniel says. 'This is a serious allegation.' He's sitting a long way forward in his chair and his hands are fists below the table, he hates meeting the unions.

'We're holding general meetings this week to decide on action,' Harry says.

'Don't threaten me,' Daniel says. He's smiling but he gets up quickly and pretends to study a painting on the wall behind us. I can't remember what it is. I think he's going to explode. My stomach feels hard. I shift around in my seat.

A nurse named Diana McGarry from the Student Health Service takes over from Harry. She has a semipermanent frown and very blue eyes that don't seem to blink often enough. 'Some of us know Gareth Ford. Some of us know the student involved. We just want to make sure the university gives him a fair go.'

Bill says, 'We're committed to finding the truth. If Gareth Ford's innocent, we'll do everything in our power to settle this thing. But we don't know yet.'

'Is it true that Gareth Ford was critical of central management in the review last year?' Harry says.

Daniel and Bill look at me. 'I don't know,' I say. 'Where did you hear that?'

'We heard the university's trying to get rid of him.'

'For God's sake,' Daniel turns around and slams his fist down on the table, it looks like it hurts. He's standing over the five of them, leaning across the table between me and Bill. 'I'm trying to manage a problem. The last thing in the world I need is for you to find a conspiracy.' Bill tries to speak but Daniel stops him. 'I don't care Bill. We're trying to move as carefully as possible on a difficult matter. And these guys are talking about grassy knolls. I just don't believe it.' He closes the door noisily as he walks out.

I'm aware the tension's been sucked out of the room with Daniel, the room fills with non-tension and the air-conditioning becomes disproportionately loud. Bill takes it calmly, tells them we need two nominees for the misconduct committee, they tell us they've nominated Harry Gutterl and Diana McGarry. They smile over at me, I smile back, dread the first meeting of the committee with them. I tell them I'll send them the papers. 'We'll stay in touch,' Bill says. 'Thanks for coming to see us before you did anything.'

They file out, look full of justified hurt. Bill says, 'They're right. We had no cause to suspend him.'

'It's only while we investigate.'

'Suspension's there for extreme circumstances,' Bill says. 'Someone who's dangerous. We've got one allegation, that's all. He's not dangerous. We're not even sure he's guilty. We shouldn't have suspended him.'

Bill goes after Daniel. I sit there soaking up the non-tension and thinking about what Bill said. Looks like I've mucked it up already, I suspended Gareth Ford when he's not dangerous enough.

# NINE

I get a call from a Mary McGrath who tells me she's acting for Gareth Ford. She has a deep rich voice, I think she must smoke. 'On what grounds is he suspended?' she says.

'We feel he could be a danger to student welfare.'

She says she'll be writing to us, I tell her my correct title and address. I tell her I look forward to her letter.

I phone the Psychologists' Registration Board and speak to the administrator there, a man named Greenacre who says there might be a claim against a registered Melbourne psychologist that the board might be investigating. But it's confidential, highly confidential. And even if there is a claim, he can't imagine they'll finish their investigation for some months, maybe a year. They don't have many resources. And these things are difficult. Very difficult. He doesn't know if he'll be able to tell me the results of any investigation they might or might not be conducting. He'll have to speak to the board chair. And the board chair is overseas. He gives me the name of a psychiatrist the board consults on sexual relationship issues. At 6 pm I catch a tram up Swanston Street to the Carlton office of Dr Hannah Kaplan.

Dr Kaplan's waiting room is in the front of a renovated terrace house off Lygon Street. The walls are a soft pink, there's a wool berber carpet on the floor, lace curtains on the windows, central heating. There's no one sitting at the small desk in the corner of the waiting room and it doesn't look as if anyone ever sits there. On the desk, there's a telephone answering machine and a small sign in thick blue handwriting that says to please sit down and Doctor will be with me soon. There are half a dozen hard-backed, raffia-seat chairs around two walls, they look as if they belong to a dining set. There's a pile of toys in one corner, unchallenging prints on the walls, pretty landscapes, flowers, ladies in long dresses. Soft classical music slips from a radio behind the desk. My mother sits straightbacked in the chair opposite me. She's crying. 'What's the matter Mummy?'

'Nothing darling.' She looks surprised.

'You look so sad.'

'Just tired.'

A young woman walks along the corridor next to the waiting room towards the exit. She's tall with very high shoes, I don't see her face. I wait another five minutes before Dr Kaplan appears. I leave my mother and follow Dr Kaplan down the corridor. I feel nervous and light. I wonder if this is what therapy is like.

Dr Kaplan looks as though she plays some sort of sport, muscles in her neck and arms and legs, relaxed rather than tense. She's wearing a red shirt and cream skirt. Her hair is dark brown and very short. I get an impression she doesn't smile easily. I feel strangely comfortable with her. She tells me she's squeezed me into her evening break, takes a white paper bag from her top drawer, and starts eating a breadroll.

The office is warm, there are tapestries on the walls, thick rugs, old chairs, cushions, orange lamps. Dr Kaplan speaks quietly except when she uses terms like *incest* or *betrayal* or *abuse* when her voice gets so loud I startle. 'It's not easy to explain,' she says, 'particularly if you don't have some experience of the therapy process. Patients are vulnerable in a way they're not in other parts of their lives. These women, and the large majority of them are women, have had the courage to trust, sometimes it's the first time they've ever trusted anyone. They're supposed to be helped. They're supposed to be acknowledged and responded to. Instead, they're abandoned, betrayed, raped by the very person they trusted.

It's shocking. I believe it's one of the worst experiences a person can have.' I notice she's wearing brown leather sandals. 'People say the client asked for it. Or why did she keep seeing him? Or if she didn't like it, why did she keep doing it? When she goes to see another therapist, chances are it will be another man who'll tell her she shouldn't complain, who might even try it on himself.'

'What about when it's mutual? Say the client and therapist agree to the sexual relationship.' Jane Kidman's claim is unclear about consent, she says she didn't really consent to sex, not the first time. She doesn't say she said no, she says she didn't say yes.

Dr Kaplan finishes a small bite of her breadroll and mouthful of water. 'What you are saying is that if the client flirts with the therapist, then it's okay.' I nod. 'I don't agree,' she says. 'Clients often flirt with their therapists, like little girls with their fathers. The important thing isn't the client's behaviour. It's the therapist's. Very few clients continue to act out sexually unless the therapist responds. It's the therapist's behaviour that matters. He has no right to get his needs met in this way in the therapy.'

'What about when therapy's finished?'

'When does therapy finish? I have clients who completed their work ten years ago who still come back now and then for top-up visits. I'm still in that role for them. I'd be very suspicious of any claim that once the weekly meetings have finished, the client no longer sees the therapist in this way.'

'But if the client agrees to sex,' I say, 'then that's their choice isn't it?'

'Again I don't agree. Therapy is about trust, it's about learning to trust someone so completely you let them in, let them help and heal. The client has no choice. The client gave up freedom of choice when she put herself in the therapist's care.'

'Do you really believe that?'

'I do. Therapy is often likened to a parent–child relationship. If it's symbolically parent–child, then sexual abuse in that context is symbolic incest.' I ask whether she'd be willing to look over Jane Kidman's claim and provide a statement. She says no. 'I'd need a consultation with the client. And I'd have to work through her therapist.' She smiles for the first time, it's not a comfortable smile. 'You don't need a statement from me. Women don't lie about these things.'

Dr Kaplan's next patient is waiting, a young woman in a navy blue blazer, one of the grammar schools I think. She looks about fifteen. She doesn't look up from her lap when I pass the waiting room. As I close the front door I hear Dr Kaplan say her name. Her voice sounds so gentle and warm I feel like turning around and asking her something but I don't know what.

I take a cab back to work. The evening light softens faces in the street. I'm warm inside the cab and I press my cheek against the cold glass. I think about Jane Kidman and my mother and the school girl in Dr Kaplan's office. I can't get out of my mind the idea that the client has no choice.

# TEN

I drive home with the Gareth Ford file on the back seat, the growing collection of letters, policy documents, newspaper reports of sexual conduct cases, a book I found in the library on counselling ethics. At home, I upend the box on the floor of the sitting room, spread paper around me, light the gas heater which glows in mauve and orange squares. I watch documents make patterns and colour the wall until I switch on a light. I walk around the mess of paper, lie down on my stomach, grab pieces at random, wonder about recombining them in a different order. Would I change the order of events? Put sex before therapy? Would it make a difference? Would I change Gareth Ford's story? The look of him? The student? The outcome? I lie there for a long time thinking. If he had sex with Jane Kidman, would it make a difference if she consented? She says she didn't really consent. Is that rape? What does not really consenting mean? If she did consent, who's responsible? She's an adult, in charge of herself. Or is she? Does he have some responsibility over and above the rest of us? Does the university have responsibility in this sense for its students? If she did consent and he had a relationship with her, what's so wrong? Trust? Breach of trust? Dr Kaplan says it's the worst experience a person can have. The girl waiting to see her when I left. Is that what happened to her?

We could dismiss him, forget the investigation, settle in the law suit, take our chances he wouldn't go after us for wrongful dismissal. There was that case in Tasmania that Daddy mentioned, I've read about it now. Professor Sydney Sparkes Orr. They dismissed him, simple, straightforward, it was misconduct for a professor to seduce his student, he seduced his student. That was the 1950s. It's different now. Civil liberties, feminism, natural justice, changing social policy. Nothing's straightforward. Differential power, staff–student relationships, codes of conduct, sexual harassment. It's not clear anymore who's supposed to protect whom. Should the university protect a 21-year-old research student from his or her 25-year-old supervisor? If one of them is 40 like Gareth Ford and the other's eighteen like Jane Kidman, is it different? Is it my job to stop them, to go after him, to punish him?

A few years ago, one of our students appealed a fail grade in a subject on the basis that her lecturer demanded sex, pinned her to his desk and stuck his tongue in her mouth, groped at the buttons of her shirt, intimated that sexual favours would be rewarded, failed her when she refused. She was firm in her written statement, cried in the interview, provided detail, buttons torn off her shirt, where his hands went, what he was wearing. She threatened to sue the university. It turned out the lecturer wasn't even in the country on the day he was supposed to have leapt on her. The student admitted lying. We took no action against her. We tried to soothe him but he was never reconciled.

The university has been trying to develop policy in this area for as long as I can remember. It took two years for the academic staff to agree there should even be a policy. Academic freedom, they kept talking about academic freedom. Now we've got a policy, it's called a code of conduct for academic staff, but years of debate have worn away its sharp edges, it's smooth and toothless, talks about what's normally expected, talks in riddles, gives excuses. Provided consent is mutual, provided you're not grading a student you're also fucking, it's really none of the university's business. It's part of life, students are not children.

Gareth Ford's not an academic staff member. Counsellors are part of my division, they're general staff, they work under different awards, different policies. Is he different from other general staff because he was her counsellor? If he was a student enrolment clerk or a gardener involved with a student, would we care? I guess not. But if he was a gardener, she wouldn't be suing us. It's certainly a breach of his professional ethics. The code of conduct for psychologists is clear. I've read it. A psychologist must not enter into a sexual relationship with a client. No exceptions.

Was something strange about Gareth Ford's appointment to the university? I grab his file and flick through again but there's nothing there. First class honours in Clinical Psychology in Adelaide, worked with welfare services, worked in private practice, worked as a lecturer at Bass University. There are internal memos on his file, applications for leave, one or two conference applications.

The phone rings and stops, rings and stops.

Jane Kidman. Could she be lying? Could she have made it up? Why? She's got nothing to gain. I can't think of a plausible reason why she'd lie about it. He must have done it. Unless she's crazy. Or unless it's money. Could anyone do something like that for money?

I gather up the pieces of paper, take them to the kitchen, sit at the table, eat some cold meat and olives. I pick up Jane Kidman's file. She's a top student who's won three prizes for her written work. Her correspondence with the university is curt, verging on smug. She's been active in the student union, edited the student paper for a year. I imagine her with black hair, bright blue eyes, large breasts, thin legs. A hard smile.

The phonebook is on the table. I find Kidman, I know the address, I dial. A well-spoken man with a voice like my father answers. I ask for Jane, my heart is thumping. She says hello. Her voice is full and young, good for court. I say hello, disguise my voice by speaking high. I say I'm from the university computer centre, I'm sorry to call her at home but we have a request from her to borrow a personal computer the next weekend.

'No.' I can hear she's smiling. 'I've got my own pc. You must have the wrong student.' She puts on an American accent as she says the wrong student. I ask if her name's Jane Kidman. 'Yeah, but I didn't ask for a computer.' She's sounds sexy like one of those ads for underwear where the girl's on the phone to the guy calling him darling. I ask if she's in Science. 'No, I'm a journalist.' She's a journalist. I say I'm sorry. When I hang up, I feel excited.

I go back to the sitting room, lie down on the floor, stare up at the ceiling. The phone rings, I think it must be Jane Kidman, she must know. I go to answer, it's not Jane, it's my friend Emily. She's talking loud and fast. She tells me she's been transferred. 'Those fuckwits don't know what they're doing,' she says. 'They won't get anyone else to work that ward.' Emily's a nurse, working with cancer patients. I ask why. 'They reckon everyone needs a break.'

'Maybe that's true.'

'I know when I need a break, not some dickhead hospital administrator. I'm the one who can decide if I'm tired. Guess where they're sending me? Spinal. Fucking spinal. Motorbike riders in wheelchairs, bike magazines, dreams of the new machine. Yuk yuk yuk.'

She asks me about work and I tell her about Gareth Ford, no names of course, but I've been thinking about him most of the day and I want to talk to someone.

'What a bad lad,' she says. 'He'll go to hell.'

I laugh. 'He sure will, he'll go down, down, down.' This was the way I talked about hell when I was little. At boarding school, Emily and I would chant, 'You'll go down, down, down' to each other whenever we did something wrong. 'I met him,' I say.

'What's he like?'

'That's the strange thing. I'm sure he did it and so I should hate him. But I don't. In fact, I think I almost liked him. He was genuine or something.'

'They're the worst, the honest ones.' I hear her light up a cigarette. 'Lot of shrinks fuck patients Adele.'

'So I've heard.'

'That's a pretty juicy job for a registrar.'

'Yeah, beats the hell out of carrying the mace at graduation ceremonies.'

'And how's Billy boy?'

Emily has met Bill Pozzi, she thinks he has kind eyes. 'He's driving me crazy,' I say. 'I'm really snowed under at the moment. This case is filling up the days and I'm supposed to be writing a big submission on quality assurance. I just feel like I'm swimming. Anyway, Bill called me down yesterday to show me a mistake in an appointment letter he'd got from HR. He'd put a little red circle around the mistake and underlined it. He said it was poor.'

'But that's not your fault.'

'Indirectly it is, it's one of my departments.'

'Did he say it was your fault?'

'Well not exactly but . . .'

'Of course he didn't. He thinks you're great.'

'He thinks I'm stupid.'

'O yeah, so why did he give you the job?'

Bill chaired the panel that appointed me as registrar. 'I just feel as if he's watching me all the time Em. Sometimes I really feel like I'm in the wrong job.'

'Adele you always do this. Remember exams? You'd come out convinced you failed. I'd think I did okay. And you always did better than me. You just don't have confidence in yourself.'

'You sound like a self-help tape.'

'No, I sound like a friend. I can't remember a time when you acknowledged you'd done something well.'

'Maybe I don't do anything well.'

'Now there's a positive self-image statement. You do lots of things well.'

'Maybe.' Emily doesn't really understand my work or what's happening. She sees everybody through this pop psychology frame where our parents are to blame for everything. And it's fine as far as it goes, but it just doesn't fit what's happening to me.

# ELEVEN

The university installed a new communication system last year. There's a microwave dish like a tiny sombrero on top of the Business Tower that sends signals to the world. Unity, that's the name of the system, like a prayer, one telephone system, one computer network, one electronic mail service.

In the first few weeks after its installation, Unity would drop out periodically. It was like the key scene in a thriller, everything went dead. The office felt hyper-real, no phones, no access to information systems, no records, no one to talk to except the people in my own building, no noise except the air-conditioning. It was the middle of the student recruitment period. We lost business. We sued the company that installed the equipment. They settled, paid to avoid the publicity.

The system cost $10 million and for that I got a new industrial grey telephone handset to replace my old cream one. I can put people on hold now and they listen to classical music, Daniel insisted on classical music. I can switch them through to other extensions and store up to 24 phone numbers in my telephone's little memory.

I'm sitting at my desk signing thank you letters to graduation speakers while I cradle the heavy receiver between my chin and shoulder like a violin. I pushbutton 2408. I know it off by heart, I have that sort of memory for phone numbers. I get the internal searching sound, that high-pitched *dddleet dddleet dddleet*, a tiny elf running along the computer cables under the floor, running up the walls to the dish on the top of the building, back down the wall on the other side, under the floor. He answers his phone. I didn't expect this, he's supposed to be suspended. He says, 'Hello?' in a soft warm way with an inflection at the end that makes him sound interested. He's not supposed to be there. I don't say anything. I've left it too long. He says 'Hello' again, then, 'It's Gareth Ford here. Who is this? Hello? Hello?'

After I hang up, I notice John standing in the doorway looking at me.

'Yes John,' I say.

'Nothing,' he says. 'I was just coming to clear the out-tray.'

At lunchtime, Bill and I are driven to the Collins Street offices of Forest and Ryan, the solicitors that act for Walters. I sit in the leather foyer watching lawyers come and go while Bill studies art on the walls. My life was like this once, I was with one of the big firms, more old-Melbourne than this one but fast in the same way at times. Some of the lawyers who emerge from within look like children. I guess I was young, too, when I started.

Their suits are so perfect, my father could never understand that anyone would want anything but a career in the law.

'Ever miss it?' Bill says.

'Never,' I say. 'You?'

'Now and then. I still consult for one or two firms.' He crosses his legs, holds his right ankle on his left knee. 'How's your father these days?'

'Not great.'

'Nothing serious I hope.'

'Not at this stage.' Suddenly I feel like crying. Of course, my father's not sick, I'm making this up, but it's as if by articulating sickness, I'm making it true.

'I didn't realise,' Bill says. 'If there's anything . . .'

'No, it's okay,' I manage to say.

Jef Blackwell's wearing a fitted dark grey wool suit with a hint of a pinstripe. He smiles and shows no teeth. He's holding a thin leather briefcase as he emerges from a large hidden door. He leads the way to the boardroom. I pull at my skirt which sticks to my legs.

Jef opens his briefcase and takes out several neatly marked plastic document holders and what looks like a miniature tape recorder but what is probably a mobile phone. 'No hope of settlement,' he says as he snaps his briefcase closed. 'They want half a million. And apologies all round.'

'At least they're starting with something reasonable,' I say.

'Yes, that's what we said.' Jef smirks and introduces a young woman who's just entered the room. She's an associate, her name is Margaret, she has long black hair, she watches Jef sweetly in the way associates watch partners, takes notes every time he speaks.

Jef briefs us on the case, mentions affidavits, evidence to date, a case budget, says we don't need to go into too much detail yet. He draws his thin lips together as if he's about to blow me a kiss. 'What have they got?' Bill says.

'They say we knew about him. We think they're bluffing.'

'Randall and Cross don't bluff.'

'Formally, they'll say nothing. Informally, they say they're confident they'll have evidence. But they won't say what.'

'Must be with a third party. Someone who's a bit nervous about coming forward. Another client?'

'I don't think so,' Jef says. 'That's the other thing I need to tell you.' Lunch is served, fish the colour of coconut-ice with a pea green sauce. There's wine too, I let the waiter fill my glass and tell myself I'll leave it undrunk but know I'll change my mind. 'There are two other clients who've made statements. They're from his private practice, they're not students. No names at this stage, there's no identifying information. We've said we want to know who they are.'

'What do they say?' Bill says.

'One claims he talked to her about sex, showed an unnatural interest in her sexual experience. The other says they developed a relationship after she'd finished seeing him as a therapist. Six months or so, they both agreed to call it off. Consensual sex.'

'But sex all the same,' Bill says. 'Doesn't sound good.'

# TWELVE

The carpark beneath the Chancellery Building has dim yellow lights. Students and staff have complained that they're afraid of the dark so we're doing something about it, installing more lighting I think. I walk to my car, my shoes echo on the gritty concrete floor. It's late.

Gareth Ford gets out of an old cream Mercedes Benz on the other side of the carpark and calls over to me. 'Adele, did you try to ring me today?'

'What are you doing here?' I feel frightened, alone, aware I'm some distance from the doors to the lift.

'Picking up some stuff.' He walks towards me quickly. 'Did you want me?'

'What?'

'I got a call from 2300 but they hung up. That's your number isn't it?'

He must have one of those phones that shows the extension of incoming calls. 'I didn't ring you.'

'That's strange,' he says. 'I was sure it was 2300.'

'Actually, I did dial a wrong number. I hung up without talking. Maybe it was you.'

He's reached me now, he's on the other side of the car door which I've opened, standing close. He smiles. 'What number were you trying to get?'

'I don't remember.' I slip the keys in the ignition, he watches me, looks beyond me to the back wall of the carpark, looks at me again, then looks inside the car. I look inside the car, too, it's a mess of clothes, newspapers and food wrappers. He's smiling. He knows I'm lying, he thinks it's funny. I don't think it's funny. I look at him again, as hard as I can manage, then slip inside the car and lock the doors as quickly as I can.

# THIRTEEN

Dr Graham Belstein runs the university's Psychology degree and answers his own phone. He has a slight mid-European accent. 'Adele, so nice to hear from you. We haven't seen you since Daryl Washington. I thought you must be on leave.'

Daryl Washington was an unsuccessful applicant for our Psychology degree who claimed one of the academic staff told him he didn't make it into the course because he was blind which would put clients off in clinical practice. 'How could I forget?' I say. 'Discrimination on the basis of disability.'

'Thank goodness you were there to fix it for us.' On Graham's recommendation, we let Daryl into the program in the end, despite the fact he wasn't qualified, because the alternative, an ugly court case, was worse. I met with Daryl, told him we'd made an administrative blunder, apologised, then forced an offer into the course.

'How is he?' I say.

'Close to the top of his year last time I checked.'

'Well, as my father says, you never know people.'

'So true, so true. I make a living out of that principle.'

I ask Graham how well he knows Gareth Ford. 'He teaches part-time in the undergraduate degree. Wonderful counsellor.' I ask if he's had any problems. 'He's a good teacher and the students like him. Does he want a promotion?'

'You've heard about the case then,' I say.

'He talked to me, yes. He wanted to know whether to

cancel his classes. I said no. In fact, I'm writing him a reference to go with his submission.'

'Do you know much about it?'

'I reviewed the case, I think he made some mistakes, but he didn't sexualise the therapy.'

'How do you know?'

'I've seen a lot of these cases. It's obvious when the client's telling the truth. And the therapists are never competent.'

'What if we're sure he did?'

'I'd want to know how you could be sure. Even so, let's assume for discussion's sake you're right. Let's assume Gareth sexualised the therapy as you say. In my view, it's a breach of ethics for a psychologist to sexualise a client relationship but that's all it is. These days we paint a picture of monster therapists preying on innocent women who have no responsibility for their actions. Relationships in therapy are no different from other relationships. Sometimes people fall in love. Sometimes they err. I wouldn't necessarily say it makes someone a bad therapist.'

'Are you saying we shouldn't take action against him?'

'I'm saying there's a way in which these things get construed as more than they are. There are strong views in many areas of life nowadays about what men should and shouldn't do and how that affects women. And it's all based on the idea that women have no responsibility for their own behaviour. I can't agree with that.'

'He has the duty of care, he's responsible for her.'

'She's also responsible for herself. She could have said no.'

'That's not the advice I've got. Do you know Dr Hannah Kaplan? She says clients aren't in a position to say no.'

'That doesn't make sense to me. I'll agree it's unacceptable for therapists or any caregivers to sexualise professional relationships. I'm not advocating any change there. Having said that, there is the notion of personal responsibility. If I'm in therapy and I have sex with my therapist, I have some responsibility for that. I'm responsible for my behaviour.'

'At eighteen?'

'Of course at eighteen. If we accept a situation where young women are not responsible for their own behaviour, how do we legislate? Where do we stop? I kissed him and touched him and said no at first then agreed to sex anyway. When we call that rape, we've gone too far. Personal responsibility gets ignored. Women become helpless victims. In Hannah Kaplan's world, women are powerless. I don't accept that.

'And at any rate, we're assuming Gareth sexualised the therapy. Which he didn't.'

'What makes you so sure?'

'It was a difficult case. I think Gareth underestimated just how difficult. In hindsight it's easy to look back over a case history and say, There, that's where I went wrong. It's harder when you're in the middle of it.' He says Jane Kidman exhibits borderline tendencies. 'It's a personality disorder of sorts. Borderlines are notoriously difficult and frustrating, it's all negative transference. She could feel he's failed her by terminating therapy. Maybe she's enraged. Maybe she decided to make up a story about him, to claim he sexualised. Or maybe she fantasised a sexual relationship.'

'You mean she believes they had sex even though they didn't?'

'It's not such a big step to start believing the things you see and hear in your head.' I know what he means. 'My feeling is Gareth should have referred her to someone else. But he didn't. He kept trying to work with her. And you'd have to say he failed spectacularly. Borderlines are generally very intelligent, they can be devious. And their rage knows no boundaries.'

At 11 am I meet with three student union executives and the university's finance manager in my office. 'It's a major commitment for students,' one of them says. 'We're getting advice.' They're getting advice. The finance manager tells them he's happy for them to get advice but the agreement's been floating round for six months. He says the university needs an answer.

We're negotiating funding for an extension to the child-care centre. We'll put up half the cost, we're offering the student union a low interest loan to fund their half, repayable over ten years. They think it's a great idea, more child care, they support us a hundred per cent. But they don't like to owe us money. In fact, they don't like to have anything to do with us.

Every university has a student union that provides services, facilities and representation. Everyone in the university community has an opinion about student unions. Student unions are bad. Student unions are good. They breed corruption. They provide services and facilities to students that the university couldn't or wouldn't otherwise provide. They're not policed properly. They work hard. Their office bearers are not accountable, they graduate before anyone sees what they've done. They provide a tremendous opportunity for kids to practise life in the world of work. Membership should be voluntary. Membership should be compulsory.

The students don't part with their independence easily. They don't want to commit to us in any way. And they don't trust our finance manager. I don't trust our finance manager. He smiles at them. 'We appreciate your position,' he says, rubbing his forehead. 'You guys have gotta make sure we're not ripping you off.' His smile is so insincere I think they'll laugh. 'But we really need to move on this. The grant can't carry over.' I don't know if this is true or not.

They promise to get back to us, within a week, with a firm commitment. When we finish I ask the union president, Andrew Fraser, to stay for a few minutes. 'I wrote to you last month about the quality submission,' I say. 'I need something in there about the union's services. I want to come and talk to your exec.'

'Anytime.'

'Fine,' I say. 'There's money in it for all of us.' I smile. Andrew's a good union president, a law student, my father would call him solid. I trust him. 'I'd also like to talk with you about a confidential matter. Do you know a student named Jane Kidman?'

'Sure, we did a drama class together. I went to a party at her place at the end of semester. Pretty weird.'

'What do you mean?'

'Her parents were overseas. There were a lot of people who weren't from uni, some of her friends are a bit strange.' He looks out the window and smiles. 'By the time I left, Jane was going from group to group asking for people's underpants. She had her own on her head and a handful of others. She said she wanted to make an underpants barbecue.'

'Were there drugs?'

'Adele, no Walters student would ever take drugs.' He's smiling.

'Do you know if Jane has a boyfriend?'

'She used to go out with a guy on the union council, Keith Marchant. Someone told me she was ugly about the split.' He stands up to leave. 'This wouldn't have anything to do with a counsellor and a mattress would it?'

'No it wouldn't.'

After lunch, the vice-chancellor walks into my office, closes the door firmly, walks over to the window, thrusts his hands in his pockets, and turns to look at me. 'I've read the paperwork on the Gareth Ford case,' he says. 'It's a nightmare.'

I tell him about the meeting with Jef Blackwell. 'They're not going to settle.'

'Worth a try. So what's happening?'

'Our committee's meeting soon.' I go over to my diary to check the date but he's not interested.

'What about the legal case?'

'They say we knew about him. I've been through the files. Central Records have been through the database looking for his name. Nothing. I don't know what they've got.' I tell him Bill thinks there must be a third party. Daniel stands at the window, looks back over his shoulder at me, as if he expects me to say something. I'm still standing at my desk looking at my computer diary. 'Maybe it's something else,' I say. 'Not correspondence. I'll check Records again but I wouldn't hold out much hope.'

'Of course, we're assuming there's something to complain about.'

'You think he didn't do it?'

'I called Des Cooper, he's VC at Bass now.' Bass is the university in Adelaide where Gareth Ford was a lecturer for five years. 'He checked him out for me. The guy won an award for his teaching, they were really sorry to lose him.

'Frankly Adele, I think we acted a bit hastily in suspending him. Bill says we had no grounds. Maybe he didn't do anything.'

'Bill's argument isn't based on whether he's innocent or guilty, it's based on a policy point, the rules on suspension, how dangerous someone is who's done what's alleged.'

'Maybe. Anyway, where are we with the other complaint the student made?'

'I met with Kit Jackson.' I tell him what Kit said about confidentiality.

He runs his hand through his hair. 'There are enough accidental situations where staff don't tell each other what's going on without creating them. I'll talk to her.' He walks over to where I'm standing. He takes up all the spare space in the office. 'Kit's really got a problem with this hasn't she?'

'She's pretty convinced he's guilty.'

'Are you?'

'Probably.'

'Well I'm not.' He's agitated. 'I think we don't know what went on. We'll never know. I thought Kit would be more mature about something like this.' He's standing close to me. He looks at me, smiles weakly. 'When I think about what this case could do to us.' I start to say I know but he goes on. 'Sometimes I feel like you and I are the only two people in this place who really understand.' He moves as if to grab my arm, then decides against it, rubs his own face instead. I want to ask what we understand but I think I should already know.

# FOURTEEN

Late in the afternoon half the university gathers in a paved courtyard for drinks to celebrate the formal opening of the Performing Arts Academy building. It has that 1990s commitment to postmodernism—brightly coloured corrugated iron, glass, unpainted concrete and minimalist landscaping. I think there are too many circles. I think I've had too much to drink.

Jack Callahan who runs Journalism at Walters is the kind of head of department who knows all his students personally. 'I've been meaning to call you Jack,' I say. 'I want some information about a student. Confidentially.'

'I've heard that one before,' he says. His voice is scratchy with an Irish–American accent. 'You'll get me in trouble with the registrar if I breach confidence Adele. And the registrar's a crazy woman.'

'That's for sure. But if you don't tell me what I want to know I'll tell the DVC we sneaked some extra students into your program this year.'

'I give in,' he says. 'What do you want to know?'

'Jane Kidman.' Jack has one of those wonderful round Irish faces that telegraphs every emotion most of the time then snaps shut. 'Just a bit of background.'

'She's a good student.'

'I can see that from her record Jack.'

'What else do you want to know?' He takes a long drink from his beer.

'Anything you can tell me.'

'She's bright, interested, works hard. She's got a good brain, knows how to use it. Writes well. Quick.' He's looking around.

'And?'

'She's like a lot of bright kids, not frightened to say what she thinks, stands up for her rights. Personally, I like that in students.'

'But?'

'Some of my people might say she's a troublemaker.'

'One of your staff lodged a formal complaint about her with the dean.'

'He overreacted.'

'What happened?'

'Jane and two other students came into his class with pillowcases over their heads. They had cap guns, they fired them a few times, then ran out. It was a newswriting workshop. They said they wanted to give the class something to write about.' He laughs. 'It was a joke.'

'When was this?'

'Early last year.' When Jane was in the middle of being irreparably damaged by Gareth Ford.

I want to ask more questions but we're joined by a group of staff, Bill Pozzi, James Goodwill from the Health faculty and Ian Preston the finance manager. In the background, a string quartet is playing something modern as if it's classical music.

'Ian says we should amalgamate with Melbourne,' James Goodwill says. He's very thin and his pelvis seems a long way forward of the rest of him.

'We're not amalgamating with anyone,' Bill says. 'We survived last time and we'll survive this time.'

Walters was fortunate during the reformation of Australian higher education of the late 1980s when the big universities acquired most of the smaller ones. Just large enough to remain independent and specialised enough to be distinctive. But there's talk of more efficiency, amalgamations. People are wary. It gets personal. 'I hope you're right Bill,' Ian Preston says. 'But we're small in the national picture. We might not survive without help this time. Which would you rather, Melbourne or Monash?' I smile, imagining Bill negotiating a job for himself at Melbourne University.

'I've got it on pretty good authority we won't be touched,' Bill says. He looks like he means it. 'They won't force mergers this time.'

'Famous last words,' says James.

'Maybe,' Bill says. He must know something.

I see Simon Radcliffe standing with a group of staff from the Performing Arts Academy. He and I dated for a while. He's laughing, his head a long way back. He's wearing a soft indigo denim jacket. He looks as if he might have been in the sun. I haven't seen him for ages.

'Huh?' I turn back to the conversation.

James Goodwill is talking. 'Graduates are like cars to you.' I've missed something important. I'm not sure what Bill said but James is accusing me. I smile, hope that's enough. It isn't. 'I get so sick of all that stuff,' James says. 'Quality submissions, strategic plans, performance indicators. They've got no idea what teaching's actually about. No idea.' Maybe he's had too much to drink.

Ian Preston rescues me. 'Adele's the registrar, not the VC. Blame Chuck for quality and planning.' Chuck is a nickname for Daniel because he's American. People laugh. We move on to the architecture. The architect is standing with Chuck on the other side of the courtyard, all bow-tie and gestures, explaining what he would have done with the right money. Bill says he thinks the Academy building looks like a child-care centre.

'Cost a lot more than a child-care centre,' Ian says.

'Haven't you read the blurb Bill?' I say. 'It's a playful, whimsical representation of academic life.'

'Bill doesn't have a playful, whimsical academic life,' Ian says.

'I think it suits the Academy to look like a child-care centre,' Bill says. 'They . . .'

I hear someone say my name. I turn around. 'Gareth.'

58

Gareth Ford. What's he doing here? I lose my spot in the conversation. I try to look around and catch Bill's eye but he's busy laughing at something. 'How are you?'

'So so.' He's wearing light blue jeans and the off-white jumper he wore the first time I met him. He looks different in the late afternoon light, maybe he's had a haircut. 'Pretty worried.' He looks down towards the concrete, hands in his pockets. 'Waiting.' I wish I hadn't drunk so much champagne. I need to make sense. 'Hope I wasn't interrupting,' he says.

'You were,' I smile. Light reaches across the courtyard in fingers that finish as glaring dots on corrugated iron, everything has that two-fast-glasses-of-champagne glow. I'm trying to be serious but I feel flippant. I look over and notice the vice-chancellor watching me. He smiles when I spot him. He thinks I'm compromising myself. I think I'm stumbling over S words.

'Have you been very involved in the quality debate?' I say to Gareth. He says he thinks it's a management fad. His eyes track mine over to the vice-chancellor.

I agree with him. I'm just about to go on when he says, 'I wish this mess was cleaned up.' I nod, unsure if he's talking about the courtyard where a lot of party rubbish is accumulating, or the case. 'I'd like to be back at work,' he says. I tell him I understand.

'Hi Adele.' It's Simon Radcliffe. He hands me a fresh glass of champagne. I introduce him and Gareth. They're about the same height or maybe Simon's a little taller. Gareth asks him which area of the Performing Arts Academy he's from.

I met Simon at an Academy performance two years ago. He asked me out after that, to the movies. Then to lunch, a few other meals, he came home for a weekend, we even went to a formal university dinner as a couple. He sort of faded out. I'm not sure what happened.

'I teach Drama in the undergraduate degree,' Simon has one of those two-day beards and thin sideburns. 'But I'm on leave at the moment. Finishing my thesis.' I convinced him to apply for professional development leave. I made sure it went through the system.

'Me too,' says Gareth. 'Working on a project.' He looks at me. 'What's your thesis about?' Simon says he's making a short film about street kids in Melbourne's bay area. Gareth says, 'Is there a thesis?'

'Yeah, the film.'

The debate in the academic board over the Doctorate in Creative Arts went on for months. The hard disciplines argued creative work couldn't be seen as doctoral level work. They talked about reflecting upon the world, contributing to knowledge, demonstrating understanding. The Arts people said their work made a contribution in a different way, they promised they reflected upon the world, they understood as much as anyone. I'm the registrar, so I stayed out of it, just gave advice on what specific proposed rules would mean. There were little thumps on the table, raised voices, shaking heads. In the end, Daniel got behind the Arts. He pushed, said we were heading for a doctoral program Beethoven would fail, talked about his experience internationally. Finally, he appealed to the authority of his office, said every now and then an institution had to indulge its vice-chancellor. The chair of the academic board resigned. Daniel appointed a new chair. They got their doctorate, a Doctor of Creative Arts, and it can be based entirely on a creative piece assessed by the relevant community.

Gareth says he wishes his masters degree could have been based on practice. 'I'd rather have done some therapy than write a thesis.' He thinks the film on street kids could be interesting. 'I worked for a few years with a homeless youth project in Adelaide.'

'Really,' Simon raises his eyebrows. 'I want the film to be powerful but I don't want to hit people over the head with it, if you know what I mean.' As he says this he gestures too widely and bumps my arm, spilling a little champagne on both of us. I say 'Sorry,' as if it was my fault. Gareth smiles at me. Simon says, 'I want it to be really something, you know?'

'Not until you tell me,' Gareth says.

'We're spending a lot of time just hanging around getting

footage. It's black and white.' As he talks he steps from one foot to the other. 'I think street kids have something special. I want to show people life on the streets, how the kids manage, group, survive. There's art in that.' He tilts his head slightly, looks up to the right as if he's thinking about something important. 'It's so good to see you Adele. You look great.'

'Kids shouldn't have to live in the streets in the first place,' Gareth says.

'It's not all bad,' Simon says. 'A lot of them move on from street life to something better.'

Gareth says it's not all good either. He's not smiling now. 'Most don't move on. I think it's easy to romanticise, but it's not at all romantic. What they have to do to survive is awful.' Simon says that he agrees but he just wants to report it how it is, not make judgements, street life is a reality and he wants to show the reality.

I notice Bill looking at me. Gareth says most media coverage of street kids is gloss. 'With the homeless youth project, we were trying to work on the real issues. But that's hard. It gets political.' Simon asks him what the real issues are. 'Most of them need long-term therapy or at least a long-term living situation where they can heal. You can't just put them in a house, give them a bath and some car engines to work on and think that changes anything. It doesn't. Eventually they have to leave.' I look over at Simon as he listens to Gareth. 'They go back to their lives, to what happens at home.'

Bill joins us. He says hello to Simon. 'I don't think we've met,' he says to Gareth. 'I'm Bill Pozzi.' He puts out his hand.

'Gareth Ford.'

Not even a flicker of recognition on Bill's face, at first I think he's forgotten the name. Then he says slowly, 'Did I see your name on a leave list?' Gareth says yes. 'Good of you to come in when you're on leave, you don't have to.' He looks at Gareth. Gareth says he likes to stay in touch. Bill smiles. 'Of course.' Then he turns to Simon. 'When are you submitting young fella?'

'End of the year.'

'Good, the Academy needs you back.' He touches Simon on the shoulder.

Gareth's standing close to me and I can feel his body along my upper arm and at my hip. I feel quite light, maybe I'm more drunk than I thought. 'I should be getting home,' I say. As I put down my glass, Simon grabs my hand.

'Let's catch up soon?'

Gareth says, 'I better go too. I'll walk out with you. Nice to meet you Bill. Hear from you soon Simon.'

'You right Adele?' Bill says.

'Fine. See you tomorrow.'

I look back at the gathering from the top of the stairs, fairy lights have just come on in all the trees and it looks like some sacred secret meeting. The string quartet has resumed after a break. They're playing something from a Peter Greenaway film, Bill Pozzi is watching me, I smile, wave, walk out of sight.

Gareth waits with me for a cab. I ask him why Simon said he'd be in touch. 'He wants to interview me for his film.'

'I must have missed that.' He asks me how well I know Simon. 'We've done a few things together. I go to the Academy's performances.'

'He likes you.' I smile. Everything seems slow and golden as if the world's in honey. Gareth asks me how someone like me wound up as a university registrar.

'That's a funny question. What do you mean someone like me?'

'You seem different from other admin people.'

I'd like to ask him what he means but I don't. 'I used to be a lawyer,' I say.

'I can't imagine that.'

'Me neither.'

He laughs. 'Why'd you give it up?'

'I was with Markham and Steiner when they were the university's solicitors. Did you know Tom McIntyre?' He knew of him. 'I used to work with him when I was with the firm. He gave me the job as university legal officer.' I pause. 'When Tom got sick, I acted in his job. When he died, they asked me to stay on for a bit. So I did. Then they advertised the position and asked me to apply. So I did. And here I am.'

'Why law?'

'My dad's a lawyer, it's a bit like that, in your blood.'

'People say you're a lot tougher than Tom McIntyre.'

'I am.'

'I would have thought you'd find it pretty hard to be tough.' He's standing close to me when he says it. I'm aware we're alone and I should probably feel frightened but I don't, I feel in charge.

'Don't be so sure,' I say. He tilts his head, smiles in a boyish way.

At home, I find mouse shit all over a breadboard on the kitchen bench and decide to set the trap Miss Bartlett gave me. I get some cheese, sit down at the table and plan the murder of my mouse.

I curl up on a chair in the sitting room watching television and listening for the snap of the trap. I feel a bit dizzy from champagne, dry in the mouth. I wonder what all this must be like for Gareth Ford and his family. We've suspended him from his job, people like me avoid him, Kit Jackson would hit him if she saw him in the street. And I have this horrible feeling that in the end, it's not going to matter whether he's innocent or guilty. It will come down to who's most believable, a young vulnerable student with a voice for TV or a middle-aged psychotherapist. My money's with Jane Kidman. But for the first time I start to wonder what the hell we'll do if he is innocent.

On the way to bed, I set off the trap myself. A dead mouse is more than I can face.

# FIFTEEN

Kit Jackson's head appears at the door. 'I'll know next time,' she says. She walks over and throws a file on my desk. 'Daniel tells me you can see anything he can see.' She's smiling as she says it but it's not a pleasant smile.

'Is this the earlier complaint from Jane Kidman?'

'Yeah,' she says as she walks out.

I call her back, get up from my desk, close the door. We're standing together behind my closed door, my hand's still on the doorknob. 'I've been meaning to call you. Were you here when Gareth Ford was appointed?'

'Before my time but I heard about it. You chaired the panel didn't you?'

'I did. There was an equity issue.' She knows this. 'Someone from your office was an observer on the panel. She said if two candidates were even we should appoint the woman.'

'That's right.'

'But they weren't even.'

'They never are. Don't tell me. She has some good experience, he has the edge. His qualifications are from a better institution. She's qualified, he's more qualified. He was more competent, more experienced, better able to carry out the duties of the position. We just had a feeling about him.' Kit is talking in a sing-song voice, mimicking every panel chair who's had to justify appointing a man over a woman in the last few years.

'It wasn't like that. He was the better candidate.'

'Doesn't seem that way now, does it?'

'We'll see. I only asked because I think I remember something. Can you ask whoever was on the panel from your office?'

'Ask them what?'

I shrug. 'I don't know, it's just when I heard his name, there was something in the back of my mind, maybe it's nothing. Just check for me.'

I throw the file across to my in-tray and go back to the quarterly financial review. John comes in, reminds me I have a meeting with the finance manager in his office. I hate meeting with the finance manager. I never know what he wants. He sits behind his desk, smiling, chatting, and then the meeting's finished and he thanks me and I think I should know why. I never do and today is no exception. By the time I get back to the office, there are phone calls to return, one more appointment, the publications manager about printing the quality submission. It's near the end of the day when I get back to my in-tray and the file from Kit Jackson on Jane Kidman's earlier complaint. There's some correspondence first that I don't read and then a report from the staff member in the equity section who mediated the complaint. This is what I want.

There was a verbal then a written complaint from a group of eight female students in a Communication subject tutorial group. The students claimed a male student brought pornographic photographs to class and displayed them. He made comments to some of the girls, or to other boys in the class, about women's bodies. Two students made a second claim, in writing, that the male student had touched his penis in class in front of them. The two students are named, one of them is Jane Kidman. I flick through the file, find their letter, it says his penis was erect and exposed.

I read on. The mediator interviewed the students as a group. She then interviewed the two students who made the subsequent claim and the boy who behaved offensively, called Ryan Laing in the report. The report says Ryan lacked understanding of the group's expectations but he had no objections to changing as soon as the offensive nature of his behaviour was pointed out to him. He agreed to counselling. The mediator recommended no further action since the second, more serious claim, of touching himself, had been withdrawn. Withdrawn. Withdrawn? I go back to the interview summaries, find the interview with the two students, the discussion. 'The students indicated their wish to withdraw their earlier written complaint. One student said she felt they might have been mistaken, that Ryan might have been doing something other than masturbating. Both students apologised for this mistake, said they were confused because they were frightened of Ryan and what he might have done if no action were taken against him.' I wonder how you could be mistaken about something like that, I wonder what Ryan was doing that looked like masturbating.

After I finish the report I close the file, imagine myself with an erect penis. I just can't see how they could mistake that.

Kit answers her phone. 'Kit, have you read this?' She has. 'The two students who made up the story about him masturbating, one of them was Jane Kidman.'

'They didn't make it up. It was a mistake.'

'A mistake? Masturbating? Do you think you could mistake something else for masturbation? They said they saw an erect penis. Kit, she's made up things before.'

# SIXTEEN

Daddy's paving under the house and wants me there for moral support. 'Jack doesn't help anymore,' he says. 'I help him but he doesn't help me.'

'Uncle Jack's not retired.'

'Just because you're retired doesn't mean your time's worthless.'

I go back to the kitchen where my mother is talking on the phone. 'Adele was just the same. Never a day sick from school.' I sit at the bench and pick up the paper. But I don't read. Mummy's conversation fades and I'm in my room in flannelette pyjamas, she's on the edge of the bed looking up at Daddy who's standing at the door, I wriggle around like a little eel. 'There there. It's all right,' she strokes my hair, there are tears in her eyes. I wish I could tell them that I'm only pretending, but it's too hard.

My mother must raise her voice on the telephone. 'If she's saying he's sick, he's sick.'

'Who was that?' I say when she hangs up.

'June Salters from the school.'

'Why were you saying I was never sick? I had weeks off school.'

'Now and then you might have had a day off.' She smiles, says brightly that I imagine things. How does she do this? She goes to the refrigerator, takes out butter, goes to the workbench, starts chopping something, I smell onion. I stay on the other side of the bench, find a pile of loose photographs. She looks over. 'Those are leftovers from the albums,' she says. 'I want to sort them.'

I take the top photograph. 'Is this Daddy's farewell?'

She squints. 'I think so.'

Daddy and his partner have their arms around each other's shoulders. Even front on, you can see Daddy's big nose, his Gallic proboscis, he says. His hair is combed back and his ears stick out. He's wearing his reading glasses which are small and goldframed, a dark suit with a white cotton shirt. He looks old. Mummy is on the other side of Daddy. She looks beautiful in a long, black evening dress. Her hair is up, she's standing too far to the left and she seems uncomfortable as if she's not supposed to be in the shot.

I flip through photographs, not really looking, until I find a shot of me as a very little baby. There's nothing to place me in scale but I look very small. I'm curled into a white sheet so my back looks like a crescent moon. My hair is black, greasy and close to my head. I have big dark eyes like those of an embryo. My belly is distended and my feet and hands, at the ends of my narrow legs and arms, are out of proportion to the rest of me, large like my eyes. I'm lying on my right side and my left hand is placed delicately in front of me in a gesture that is very like one of my mother's when she's showing surprise, wrist bent over, index and middle finger pointing slightly. It looks out of place. My facial expression is hard to read. 'Here's one of me in hospital,' I say.

She looks over, squinting, then puts her knife down, walks over to the other side of the bench at which I'm sitting and peers at the photograph. 'No, that was here in the nursery.'

'It doesn't look like it,' I say. 'There's something behind me that looks like a hospital bed.' She doesn't reply. 'Are there any photographs of me in hospital?'

'I don't think so.'

'But I was there for months.'

'We were worried all the time. I didn't think about taking pictures.' She walks over to the workbench and picks up her knife.

'What did I nearly die of?'

'You were premature, too little, you know that.' She turns around and looks at me.

On Sunday, Uncle Jack and I sit on the back verandah of his house and look at the steel blue water of Bass Strait. The others are inside. 'Do you remember the bird catcher?' I say.

'Sure do,' he says. 'A fruitbox, a stick, a piece of string and something sweet as a lure.'

'We never actually caught anything Jack.'

'Are you saying the pigeon was not a bird?'

'Fell out of a nest.'

'You know, I think you're right.'

'It fell out of a nest and I asked you where babies came from.'

'That's right, you did, and I blushed.'

'I don't remember that, but you didn't tell me.'

'Well no.'

'Will you tell me now?' We laugh.

Daddy joins us. 'I read your case file this morning,' he says. 'Where are you with it?'

'The committee's meeting next week.'

'What's this?' says Uncle Jack.

I start to reply but Daddy cuts in. He had a lot of red wine with lunch. 'It's that case Adele's involved in, the counsellor accused of sex.'

'It's not as straightforward as I thought,' I say. Daddy asks what I mean. 'We have a written allegation from the student and a denial from the counsellor. At first, it seemed obvious he did it. Now I'm not so sure.'

'I told you, innocent until proven,' he thrusts an index finger at me on each word.

'It's not that simple,' I say. I haven't told him about the Ryan Laing complaint, Jane Kidman's lies. 'At first I thought no one would lie about something like this. But maybe they would.'

'What's your evidence?'

I think about this. I'd assumed he did it, of course he did, she has no reason to lie, he was alone with her over months and months, her submission's so convincing. Gareth Ford seduced Jane Kidman. So what have I been doing? Conducting an investigation with an unbiased view? No. I've been testing my theory, seeing whether it will stand up in the committee, poking and prodding to see if it works. Sure, I've talked about being objective, chastised people like Kit Jackson for bias, but when it comes right down to it, I've never been in doubt. He did it. I even got him suspended on the strength of my beliefs. I didn't know if I could prove it, but I was sure he did it. Daddy's right, I've assumed he's guilty all along.

And I thought the committee would probably find him guilty too. Kit's going to go for him no matter what we turn up. My best guess is the chancellor who'll chair the committee thinks he's guilty on the grounds that middle-aged men seduce young girls. And the two staff, maybe they'll stick by Gareth. Maybe not. And me? I'd already figured it out. Jane Kidman's young, talented, bright, the future. She's hurt. Gareth Ford's older than her and a bit strange, he has strong views, there are question marks.

Almost in spite of myself, what I've actually found out is that Gareth's not strange, he's decent, a good staff member with friends among his colleagues, active in his profession, well regarded, points to a number of success stories with our students. And Jane Kidman? Jane Kidman's a smart student who's been in trouble, nothing serious, but trouble all the same. She's a bit wild, life's pretty easy for her. She tells lies.

Daddy's been talking. 'In the States this is the most common dispute between therapists and patients,' he says. He leans over to me. 'But he must have done it Adele.'

'Why?' I must have missed something.

'Her statement's too detailed. She's been those places she talks about.'

'Maybe.' He's making the same assumptions I made.

'I'm not saying you can prove it, I don't think you can. I don't think you've got a hope, looking at your evidence. I think he has to get off because you'll never know what happened and there's no way to find out.' He gulps his wine.

'I've got a feeling you're wrong. I'm not sure he'll get off, but I'm not sure he did it either. What if I were to say we have some evidence she's lied about something like this before?'

'Doesn't matter,' he says. 'You make too many assumptions about people. You've got to look at the facts, the evidence Adele, and make your decision on that basis.' I make too many assumptions, what about him? 'Why do you think he's innocent?'

'I didn't say he was innocent. I said I wasn't sure. I might change, I might find more information. I didn't say he was innocent, I just said things change.'

# SEVENTEEN

The university public affairs director, Mark Campinelli, is standing in the doorway of my office. He's short and solid like a wrestler. He wears a vest with a gold chain in the pocket that probably isn't connected to a watch. He has large cream teeth and black hair combed back like a wet seal. He's excited and talking too fast. 'The student paper's got a two-page spread so we're really in it now. I've had three calls already.'

I call out to John. 'I need a copy of *Yarra*,' the student union newspaper. I turn back to Mark. 'Have you drafted a statement?'

'Yeah, but I can't get in touch with Daniel. I've put your name down for inquiries. Will you have a look at it?'

The statement's good, Gareth Ford is a university employee, the university's governing council is aware of a number of unproven allegations, we're investigating, we won't take action until the investigation's finished. I make one or two changes to the language, change the statement that Gareth's suspended to say that he's on leave, and give it back to Mark for dispatch.

John returns with *Yarra*. It's a big story, front page pointer to pages four and five. The headline reads 'And gladly leche'. Why Chaucer? Gareth Ford's not even a teacher. They've included one of our newspaper ads from *The university that values students* campaign. They've scrawled out *values* and written *fucks* in red. *Walters, the university that fucks students.*

They've talked to students who've seen Gareth as a counsellor, who think he's weird. No names. They say we declined to comment and we're keeping him on staff even though we know he took advantage of students. I note the plural. Jane Kidman didn't want to be interviewed. There's a photograph of Gareth, God knows where from, a full page close-up, he's eating something, I think it's a hamburger, the shot's grainy, he looks like a war criminal.

For the rest of the day I respond to the press. Yes, we're aware of the allegations, yes we're investigating, no we haven't dismissed Mr Ford, yes Mr Ford has been suspended until the matter's cleared up. Mr Ford's been with us for nearly three years. Based on regular performance review, he's doing a fine job. No, we haven't sacked Mr Ford. We wouldn't sack someone on the basis of unproven allegations. Yes, I understand there's a court case. Yes the university is joined in the suit. No, we won't be releasing the name of the student involved. The vice-chancellor will be back tomorrow and available for interview.

Late in the afternoon, Bill Pozzi comes into my office without knocking. 'The Gareth Ford thing's out.'

I freeze. 'I thought Mark called you. We put out a statement. I think it's all right.'

Daniel calls me at home. 'Sorry to ring so late, Mark said the Ford case hit the press.'

'I got quite a few calls today,' I say. 'No TV tonight but I think we might get in the papers tomorrow.' I'm squinting in the light I've just switched on.

'Thanks for handling things, you did a great job.'

The next morning Mark says we've hosed it down. 'Three pars in *The Age* and five in *The Herald*,' he says.

'They're probably waiting to run a big story after our council meeting,' I say. 'But it's breathing space.'

Gareth calls me. 'My lawyer said to say no comment.' I tell him I'll send him a copy of our statement. 'I could sue the student union for defamation,' he says.

'That's up to you. More press won't be good for any of us.'

'I feel so bloody powerless.'

After lunch, the vice-chancellor and I meet with Andrew Fraser and the *Yarra* editors. Daniel talks about professional ethics, responsibility, truth and allegations. 'I understand how you feel Andrew, but you can't go around saying something's a fact until it's proven.'

'We're getting complaints from students,' Andrew says. 'If he didn't do anything, why are people saying he did?'

Daniel smiles. 'That's hardly relevant. If I tell you something, it doesn't make it true. In fact, it generally means you don't believe it.' Andrew smiles. 'We're investigating. Believe me, you'll be the second to know if Gareth Ford's done something wrong.'

'Who'll be the first?'

'He will. I'll sack him.'

We get a guarantee the students won't publish another story about Gareth Ford without checking with me first. They won't stick to it, but it's the best we can do.

# EIGHTEEN

The management group meets in the conference room at Walters House, fourteen men and me sit around a table under quartz halogen lights. Daniel chairs. 'Item 3 is the quality submission. Adele, where are we?'

'Everyone has a copy.' I hold up mine, 'This version, with a few editorial mods, is with the printing section. It's due in Canberra at the end of this week.' Two of the faculty deans opposite me are carrying on a conversation and laughing softly. 'We're very strong in particular areas. Library, study skills, career and personal counselling.' Daniel and I exchange looks. 'I'm pretty happy with the submission overall. Still a lot of work to do before the committee visits us.'

Daniel tells them the date of the visit. 'It's a team of five,' I say. 'I've attached names and brief CVs to the papers. No surprises in terms of who they want to see during the day. Groups of ten, lots of students and support services staff. My office is organising the program. A couple of deans are involved. We'll be in touch with everyone for suggested names.'

'How long they coming for?'

'A day,' I say. 'Same as the last few years. Eight sessions. They want lunch alone.'

'Adele's done a mighty job to pull this together,' Daniel says. 'Few months ago, I'd have said we didn't have a chance. Now I think we're one of the highest quality student service institutions in the country. Big day for everyone coming up. Top work Adele. I don't know how you do it, but you've done it.'

Daniel takes the opportunity to brief the management group on Gareth Ford. 'We're doing everything we can to sort it out quietly. Adele, Bill, you want to add anything.'

Bill says it's an unusual case. 'With an academic staff member and a student the ethics are less clear. Most academics would say they have a right to whatever relationships they want. And that's true in law. In this situation, we're talking about a professional psychologist whose ethics clearly prohibit relationships with clients.'

One of the deans asks what outcome is likely. 'He denies the claim,' I say. 'So we're investigating.'

Daniel tells them he'll keep them posted.

After morning tea, we discuss changes to a scheme to help women in their academic careers by providing time off on full pay to study for a higher degree. One of the faculty deans says the scheme discriminates against men. 'Women have had every opportunity to catch up now. How long will we keep these sorts of schemes going? Surely it's time to move on.'

Another agrees. 'There's a lot of unrest in my faculty. There are highly qualified women abusing schemes like this. I'd prefer we targeted specific needs than run a blanket scheme that can be abused.'.

I'm the only woman at the meeting and one or two members are looking at me as if they expect a response. But I'm silent. I have no moral centre. My father told me that when I was seventeen and he caught me lying. I'd been to an Adam Ant concert with Emily but I'd said that I was at her place. He found the ticket in my desk drawer. He was disgusted by me. 'How could you do this? How could you do this to your mother?' I couldn't answer him. I couldn't respond to the deans.

Bill Pozzi says we should support the scheme. 'Women have caught up? I don't see too many high powered senior women around this table. We have to recognise disadvantage in career development. Doctoral enrolments nationally are still skewed. This scheme provides women with an opportunity to make up for lost time. I think it's imperative.'

Daniel agrees. They approve the scheme.

# NINETEEN

Emily lights a cigarette. 'How old is she?'

'Twenty,' I say. My best friend Emily has small black eyes and her face is sort of fuzzy with fine fair hairs. She's not very tall, maybe five foot one, she has a toothy smile and sometimes I look at her and think of a wombat. We're sitting at the counter at Pellegrini's which is crowded and full of cigarette smoke. It's raining outside. I've got apple strudel with cream, coffee in a tumbler. Emily doesn't eat sweets.

'She's just a kid,' she says.

'So?'

'Maybe she likes making things up.' She smiles. 'I told the nuns once a guy flashed at me at the railway station.'

'I thought that was true.'

'I saw a guy in a raincoat, but he didn't do anything.'

'What if they'd charged him?' I say.

'I didn't think about it.'

'Why?'

'I wanted to be important.' She takes a sip of her coffee. 'Maybe your student wants to be important too.'

'It's the worst thing I've ever been involved in. I got his written response today. He says touching and caressing are part of his therapy. Is that what you did?'

Emily in therapy was like one of those people who do triathlons. Her little dark eyes would dart all over the place, she'd use her hands to talk, grab me by the arm as if everything was urgent. 'Therapy was the best thing I ever did, I was such a mess.' I'd never thought of Emily as a mess, at school she was always the one in charge. Actually, she was more of a mess when she was in therapy. She said she was working through some hard issues to do with her family, she asked me to be patient, and I was, but therapy didn't seem to be helping. She got really depressed. Then when she did start to feel better, she used to hug everybody, people she hardly knew. She even hugged Daddy. She didn't stay like that, eventually she seemed more like her old self. But different, too. Now she's larger, sometimes she takes up too much space. When she smiles, her teeth show. She drinks her coffee as if she's attacking it.

'But what did you actually do in the sessions?'

'Talked.'

'Did you ever feel your therapist was coming on?'

'Never. Dwight told me he loved me once, but it wasn't a come on. Mind you, there was a stage where I think I might have liked it if he did.'

'What do you mean?'

'It's hard to explain if you haven't been through it. I thought he was wonderful. He seemed to have what I needed. I used to think about him all the time. So, if he'd come on sexually, I think I'd have treated that as pretty good news.'

'You told me he was an ugly old man.'

'He was.'

'Did you flirt with him?'

'Maybe a bit,' she says. 'It wasn't really sex I wanted. I wanted him to care about me.'

'Did you lie on the floor?' As soon as I ask this question, I wish I hadn't, but Emily doesn't seem to notice.

'Yeah, regressive work. He used to wrap around me while I cried.'

'How did it help you?'

Emily looks at me and doesn't answer straight away, she takes her coffee glass, holds it in her two hands, puts it down again. 'It's about trust.' She pauses again. 'I always thought I'd find this big thing wrong with me and that when I found it, I'd be better. I went on for ages in therapy thinking this. But what I really needed to do was simple. I needed to trust someone. Once I could trust one person, I knew life was different from how I'd learned it was. It was very simple really, but it took a long time.'

While Emily's been talking, I've been making a mess by cutting into the cream on my plate with my coffee spoon. She asks me what Gareth's like. 'At first, I thought he was a bit of a creep, one of those people who says nice things they don't mean, touches everyone, gazes into your eyes. But there was something about him I liked, something that seemed genuine. Now, I think it's for real. He's decent Em, talks about all the right things, homeless people, kids. He cares, you can tell he cares. Everyone likes him, the other counsellors, academic staff, students he's worked with. I think she's lying.'

'Why?'

'Revenge, money, I don't know. She's lied before. She's pretty crazy.'

'I'd have been called crazy once.'

'No you wouldn't.'

'Yes I would. And I really would have been crazy if Dwight had screwed me. Do you think he'll get off?'

'Daddy says he should, I should look at the evidence, what I know to be true. He's innocent until proven guilty Adele.' I do my best to imitate my father's voice.

'That sounds just like your dad,' she says. 'How are they?'

'I've been going down most weekends, they're getting old.' She smiles. 'What?'

'You're 30 Adele, and you're still going home from boarding school every weekend.'

'It's not like that. I want to visit them. Not everyone hates their parents Emily.'

'No, and I don't hate my parents. But I don't live their lives either.' This really annoys me about Emily, it's one of the things she started doing when she was in therapy, I call it her voodoo doll approach to life.

She smiles and puts her hand on my arm. 'I'm sorry, tell me to shut-up.'

'Shut-up.'

'I will. But don't you just wish a little bit that you didn't have to do everything they want?' She smiles.

A woman sits down next to me, she has black hair cut close around her face, bright green eyes and white skin. She looks like a cat. Behind her my mother is looking at me, silent, letting me know she disapproves. 'I've had this really weird feeling lately,' I say. 'As if the whole world's operating in code only I don't get it. My parents get it, and the people I work with, even you. But not me. Sometimes I think if I only knew the code, I'd be all right, I'd know.'

'Know what?'

'Something.' I turn to look for my mother but she's gone. 'Do you ever talk to yourself?'

'All the time.'

'Conversations?'

'Yeah.'

'People answer?'

'What, when they're not there.'

'Well not physically there.'

'I guess not. Do you?'

'I don't know.' I drain my glass. 'Let's get out of here.'

# TWENTY

I'm the Easter bunny. I take Easter eggs from my basket and hand them to chocolate-faced, sticky-fingered small children. I swing my rabbit head and shoulders from side to side as I walk like Dorothy's friends on the road to Oz. I trip on my rabbit-foot shoes. My rabbit ears fall in front of my eyes. My rabbit hips, at my knees, are wider than my real hips. I'm pear shaped, more like Humphrey B Bear than a rabbit. I wouldn't have chosen to be a rabbit. I wouldn't tell my father I'm a rabbit.

For all the years he was university registrar, Tom McIntyre was the Easter bunny at the child-care centre at morning tea on the last work day before Easter. When he got sick and I was acting registrar they asked me to fill in. I was going to say no, I thought it was ridiculous, I wasn't Tom, I'd look silly in a rabbit suit. But I've always been impulsive and something made me say yes. So now I'm the Easter bunny. I was right, I do look silly in a rabbit suit.

Some of the children are scared of me, I'd have been scared of me when I was a little girl. I respect their fear, don't go too close, do funny things with my arms and legs, leave chocolate at a safe distance. Eventually they wander over, look closer, take the chocolate, withdraw. Other children, the Emilys of this world, come up behind me and pull my tail, yank my ears when I bend down to them. The staff think it's great.

The public relations people wanted to take photographs. Mark Campinelli pleaded. 'Your human side,' he said. 'It will be great in *Walters News*.'

*Walters News* is the staff newspaper. 'No Mark. I don't mind being a bunny in a silly suit to make kids laugh. But no photographs.'

Gareth Ford walks in holding the hand of a small child. I hide behind the play gym equipment but he sees me and walks around it. His daughter, who looks about three, hides behind her father. 'Are you okay Hilary?' he says. She shakes her head no. He bends down, puts his arms around her, says something I miss. He looks up to me. 'She's frightened of the bunny. Do you think it's an omen?'

'No, you know what bunnies are like.' I have a feeling my voice comes out of this suit like a megaphone.

'Do I?' He picks Hilary up and says to her, 'It's a pretty scary bunny, honey.' She giggles. 'Do you reckon Daddy could pat her on the ear?' She shakes her head no, but she doesn't look as frightened, she's half smiling now that her father is holding her, as if the bunny isn't dangerous and this is a game. 'Daddy might try.' She nods yes. He puts his hand out slowly. She looks excited, her eyes dart from his hand to his face. He touches my left rabbit ear and withdraws his hand quickly, watching Hilary all the while. I try to appear friendly, there's not much flexibility for expression in a six-foot rabbit suit. Gareth repeats this exercise several times until finally, Hilary decides to touch my ear herself. He leans over with her, his face is very close, I can see his eyes, I can look hard at them because he can't see mine through my suit. When she finally touches my ear Gareth says to her, 'I don't think it's a scary bunny at all. I think it's a friendly bunny.' He looks straight at my eyes behind my whiskers, as if he knew where they were all the time. Hilary's laughing, Gareth's smiling while he's looking at me, I want to look away, but I don't, I go on looking. 'There's Trent,' he says to Hilary. He puts her down, takes off her knapsack and hat and she runs over to the sandpit.

'Thanks for that. She likes to test scary things.' He says it's a great suit. I say thanks a lot. 'I'm serious. It's great you do this.'

'To tell the truth, it's fun.'

We stand there for a moment among noisy children. 'I better let you get back.'

'I'm just about finished,' I look for my watch and see my grey rabbit paw. He says it's nearly eleven. 'I clock off at eleven. I want to talk to you about something. You got time for a coffee?'

'Sure I got time.'

I finish scattering eggs, wave goodbye to the kids who've lost interest in me by now anyway, change, go back to my office, give my pelt to John and tell him I have to go out for a couple of hours. He asks where. I tell him it's personal business. He looks hurt, he doesn't like me to do things he doesn't know about.

We meet at Southgate, Gareth's standing outside the coffee shop when I arrive, it's an overcast day and cold but it doesn't look like rain. We sit outside, looking across the crowded forecourt down to the brown river. I don't like this coffee shop but it was the only one we both knew straight away. The staff wear black. They act as if making coffee is something they don't have to do, it's something they choose to do, something they might not do for me. They move aimlessly, whisper to each other and laugh, look at me as if there's something wrong with me. They don't like me. 'I hate this coffee shop,' Gareth says. 'The staff are awful.'

'Me too.' I nearly say I was thinking the same thing but I don't for some reason. I must be smiling though because he says, 'What?'

'I was thinking the same thing.' He says snap. I say what. He says snap, the card game, when you see the same thing twice, snap. I'm not sure what he means. He sits up in his seat, says when two things are the same, you say snap, just like in the card game. I say oh. He says you had to have a snap childhood. I laugh. 'Did you have a snap childhood?' I say.

'Snap, canasta, five hundred, bridge. We were a card family. How about you?'

'Chess, but I'm no good at it.'

'Me neither. I can never remember which pieces make which moves. I bet your father's a good chess player.'

'He is. He used to try to teach me but he's given up now.'

Gareth doesn't say anything about us meeting outside the misconduct process, perhaps he doesn't think it's strange. Perhaps I'm the only one who thinks things like that are strange. Maybe it's because I'm a lawyer.

'Your father's a lawyer, isn't he?'

I nearly say snap but then I'd have to explain. 'Retired.'

'My dad was a minister. I bet our childhoods had a lot in common.'

'Probably.' There's a pause. 'I read your submission.' He says good. 'I've been thinking.' I wait, he's looking at me, his mouth is closed, his eyes are really bright, maybe they look brighter on grey days. 'I think I believe you.' He swallows but doesn't say anything. 'It doesn't mean anything,' I press my palms flat against the air. 'And I'm not saying I won't change my mind. I haven't seen all the evidence yet. But based on what I have seen, I believe you.' I don't tell him about Ryan Laing and Jane Kidman's lies.

The forecourt where we're sitting is thick with pre-lunchtime workers in suits. Pasted on the soft Melbourne light, they dominate the scene as they hurry to important appointments eating takeaway from white paper bags or talking into small black mobile phones.

'I'm so relieved,' he says. I tell him again that my view might change, there's more evidence to come in, I'm only one person on a five-member committee, we won't know the outcome until we know it. He says he understands all that. 'It's not that I think you're going to get me off. I appreciate your position, I really do. It's just that until now, no one believed me.' I tell him I disagree, a lot of people support him. 'They might when they talk to you. But they avoid me. If I ring, they keep a distance, just in case. Even people I'm really close to. It's a shadow, enough to make them wonder.

There are one or two people who've stood by me right through. But I'm just so glad someone like you believes me.'

One of the cafe staff saunters towards us. Gareth signals so obviously, waving with both arms, that she can't avoid us. When she reaches us, she looks out to the water while she asks what we want. Her earrings are huge gold concentric circles and she keeps touching them. We order coffee, she sighs, doesn't say anything, it's a huge problem. As she walks away, I look over at Gareth and we both burst out laughing. He shrugs. I return the gesture.

'That's all I wanted to tell you really,' I say. 'I probably shouldn't even say that much.' Damned right I shouldn't. The correct position is that I'm impartial and he's accused. I'm not supposed to think anything until the very last hour of the last day of the investigation. And if I do think anything, he's the last person to whom I should disclose it. But I feel bad I assumed he was guilty, I feel bad I told Daniel to suspend him, I feel bad about what he must be going through. Daddy was right. Based on the evidence, we shouldn't find him guilty. And more than that, everything in me tells me he's innocent.

Coffee arrives, it's been spilled in the saucer, it clatters onto the table but it tastes good. Gareth breathes in and out from his shoulders, says well. I say well too. 'How old is Hilary?' I say.

'Two.'

'She's tall.'

'Like her dad,' he says. 'She's wonderful.' I nod. 'Also like her dad.' I smile. I ask if his wife works. 'We're separated. Christine's gone back to Adelaide.' I say I'm sorry, I didn't know. 'Hilary lives with me.' I ask if Christine works. She's a graphic artist. 'What about you,' he says. 'Are you in a relationship?'

I used to be asked this question by my mother, my mother's mother, my mother's sisters and my mother's friends. Is there anyone, dear? Someone special? A beau? A pretty thing like you must chase them away. Are you bringing someone?

What's his name, dear? What does he do? Who is he? Used to drive me crazy. 'No, just me.'

'What about Simon?'

'We went out a few times, then we sort of drifted.'

'I bet anyone you brought home wouldn't be good enough for your dad.'

'He's not like that.'

'Maybe our childhoods weren't so similar. What is he like?'

'Clever.' I tell him I'm an only child, my parents are older, they were strict when I was little, especially my father, but I don't mind that. I tell him I think sometimes parents are not strict enough. He listens, says he finds that interesting. Then he asks if I was scared of my father. I tell him I don't need therapy. He laughs, doesn't say anything. I think about his question. 'Yeah, I guess I was a bit scared of him sometimes. Sometimes, I'm still a bit scared of him.' I poke a face, laugh as I say it. He doesn't laugh, he just looks at me with gentle blue eyes. He takes a packet of cigarettes out of his top pocket, lights one. I didn't know he smoked. We sit there for a few moments, he smokes his cigarette, I think of how sophisticated I could be if I smoked. Finally, more to break the silence than anything, I look at my watch. 'I'd better get back to work.'

He stands on his cigarette and thanks me. 'They say there's a special sort of intimacy between the torturer and the tortured. Maybe the same goes for the investigator and the investigated.'

'Maybe.' He's standing close to me, I seem to have moved around the table near to where he was sitting. We're about the same height because of my boots.

'Can I give you a hug?' he says. I say yes but his face reminds me of Emily's when she asks, too friendly, I feel as if he might eat me. When he does hug me it's gentle. He says thanks again. 'I'm so glad you're the one.' He steps back. I want to ask him what he means about me being the one but then he's walking away.

# TWENTY-ONE

There's a telephone message from Helen Yates in Central Records. 'You know those names you gave me to search for?' she says when I call back. I'd asked her to look up Gareth Ford and his former employers in the correspondence database. 'Well I found some.' Helen's found letters from Bass University where Gareth worked previously and from the hospital where he held a joint appointment.

'Anything that looks interesting?' I say. John brings a letter over to me to sign, apologising to a student whose graduation parchment we lost. I read while I talk to Helen.

'What do you mean interesting?'

'Anything that looks like it could be a complaint about counsellors, especially if it's got a name like Gareth Ford.'

'There weren't any records under Gareth Ford.'

'I know that Helen but maybe they got the spelling wrong or something.'

'Gareth Ford? How could you spell Gareth Ford wrong?'

'I don't know. I just want you to check, okay?' I should go down to Records and check myself but I don't have time. I sign the letter and give it back to John. 'Who files referee reports for staff appointments?'

'HR,' Helen says. The human resources department. 'They're kept in archives. I think they destroy them after two or three years.' I say thanks, I'll call HR.

I call out to John. 'Are we sending that graduate her parchment now?'

'By courier.'

'Good. Call her and tell her it's coming. Apologise on my behalf.'

I call Jim Berry from HR. He doesn't like me. He wishes I hadn't been made registrar. He wishes he had been. 'Did you get my note?'

'Gareth Ford. You were right. We appointed him three years ago. You chaired the panel. It was straightforward. He was the best candidate, met the selection criteria and then some. There was a second appointable candidate and we would have made an offer if Ford hadn't accepted. You've got his personal file. It's clean. His probationary report is fine.'

'What about the referee reports when we appointed him?'

'I think they'd have been destroyed by now. I'll check archives and get back to you.'

'Good.' Why do I keep thinking I remember something?

John is leaning a long way back in his chair to look at me through my door, he's put the phone on hold. 'It's your father,' he says.

'Put him through.' Daddy says he's ringing about the weekend.

'I'll be up on Saturday.'

'Good love.' There's a long gap.

'How's Mummy?'

She's well. His voice fades as if he's not holding the receiver properly. 'How's that case coming along?'

How come he never asks about anything else, like the admission round or graduation ceremonies? Why do I always have to be a lawyer? 'I don't think there's enough evidence to find him guilty.'

'That's what I said.' That's what I said. Drives me mad.

'And I'm not sure he did it.'

'You'll never be sure.'

'I think he didn't do it. I think she's lying.'

I expect this will prompt an outburst about objectivity and subjectivity. Instead, he clears his throat, says gently. 'Be careful love. Cases like this are nothing but trouble.'

'How's the paving?'

'Nearly done.' I can hear a smile in his voice. 'What time on Saturday?'

I get off the phone as soon as I can. He sounds so old. I hate it when he's nice to me.

# TWENTY-TWO

The misconduct committee meets in the council chamber, one of the oldest rooms in Melbourne, the original dining room of Walters House, the university's only sandstone building and the former home of Sir James Jeffrey Walters after whom the university is named. I wanted somewhere with artificial light and a big table between me and the people I have to meet. I wanted distance from the rest of the committee, especially Kit. I wanted space to think.

Chandeliers hang useless and beautiful from the ceiling in the council chamber, augmented by subtle but effective halogen lamps. The floors are polished maple and there are two fireplaces with carved mantelpieces. There are French windows covered with rich dark curtains along one wall. Along another wall there are display cabinets full of university regalia, the mace, shield, robes and gavel. The council meeting table is the original Walters dining table, it seats 30 and eight strong people can barely lift it.

The chancellor whose main job is to chair the university's governing council is Dr Sir Charles Hindmarsh, a retired obstetrician. The skin on his face is pink and looks as if it's covered in fine white powder. When I called him and asked for a council nominee to chair the misconduct committee he nominated himself.

It's like a funeral. I introduce Gareth. I tell him to sit down opposite the committee which sits in a line facing the door. We're like a group of sad game-show contestants. The secre-

tary, blackrimmed glasses, green shirt and coloured tie, pieces
of paper fanning out over the table. Me, sitting straight, navy
suit, hands but not elbows on the table. Kit, sitting forward,
eyes on Gareth. Sir Charles, white shirt, black suit like a judge.
The staff nominees—Harry Gutterl who looks as if he's the
one who's been charged, impossible to read, and Diana
McGarry who knows Gareth.

Gareth's wearing different glasses, round brown rims, his
eyes look irritated. His hair's combed and stuck down with
something. Why hasn't he brought his lawyer?

Sir Charles begins. 'Mr Ford, the purpose of this interview
is to enable my committee to ascertain the facts from your
point of view in relation to your relationship with student
Jane May Kidman.' In relation to your relationship? He's
going to be unbearable. He talks slowly and his voice is muted
as if it's coming up through water or foam. It drifts off into
the large room. 'The committee will ask questions and then
there will be time for you to make a statement if you wish.'
Gareth agrees to the process. 'This a very serious matter.'
Gareth nods, breathes in and out, he's looking over at Kit, he
seems nervous. I look at Kit, too, she's glaring at him.

Sir Charles is warming up. 'You say in your statement that
Jane Kidman came to you for counselling and saw you once
or twice a week for just over eighteen months. Is that correct?'

'Sometimes she saw me three times a week.'

'And could you describe for me the complaint she pre-
sented with?'

'Provided I have an assurance about confidentiality.' Gareth
looks at the secretary.

'Certainly,' Sir Charles looks at me. I lean over, nudge the
secretary who puts down his pen. We smile at each other.

'Jane was depressed when she first came to see me, she'd
attempted suicide some months earlier.'

'A serious attempt?'

'I don't think there's any such thing as an unserious
attempt at suicide.' Gareth looks as if he's going to explain,
then thinks better of it. 'She was acting out, drinking, drugs,
she'd hurt herself a couple of times, accidents that might not

have been completely accidental. I felt the best course of action was to help her understand the source of her depression and work on that.'

'What was your diagnosis?'

'Jane comes from a background of child abuse. She had very little sense of her self. She felt not good enough at the very core of her being.'

'She claims that over time, you became increasingly familiar with her. Is this true?'

'I'm her therapist. Part of therapy is building trust. It's hard to trust someone who isn't familiar to you.'

'She says your sessions involved you lying on the floor on a mattress with her and kissing her. Is this correct?'

There's a discernible air-conditioner hum in the gaps between questions and answers. 'Jane did a lot of regressive work with me.'

'Is her statement correct?'

'Yes, it's correct, but it's not the way I'd put it. We did a lot of regressive work.'

They all react to this, even the staff reps. Sir Charles says, 'You're telling me you lay on a bed and kissed Jane Kidman?'

'Let me explain.' Gareth sits forward, spreads his hands in front of his chest in a stop-there gesture.

'No need to explain Mr Ford. How many times did you hold Jane Kidman in your arms or lie on the floor together?'

'Most sessions.'

'Mr Ford, did you make any sexual advance towards Miss Kidman at any stage?'

'No I did not.'

'Did you have sexual intercourse with Jane Kidman?'

'Absolutely not.'

'Did you engage at any time in any form of sexual contact with Jane Kidman?'

'No.'

'Mr Ford, in your job, you must get close to your clients.' Sir Charles smiles at Gareth like a prosecution lawyer about to pounce.

'Yes I do and it's something I'm proud of.'

'And in the case of Jane Kidman, you've told us that you had physical contact every session.'

'Yes, that's in my written statement.'

'Did you have sexual feelings towards her?'

'Not like I would for a woman.'

'Just answer the question.'

'No, not that I acted on.'

'I don't understand.'

Gareth looks away up to the right. I watch my cream hands on the dark wood tabletop. 'It's a bit like a mother breastfeeding. When I'm doing regressive work, the client is like a small child. I don't think of her as a woman lying there with me. I see her as a little person. So it's the same as a mother who can be quite sexually stimulated by a baby breastfeeding. But she doesn't have sex with her baby.'

A ripple of discomfort moves along the line of committee members, it's not a great analogy from Gareth's point of view. 'There's an important difference between a baby and Jane Kidman,' Harry Gutterl says. 'Your patient isn't a baby. She's a young woman.'

'Maybe she's that to you. But when I was working with her, she was a little child. I held her while she regressed. She did some good work.'

'And in all that time, you never had sexual feelings towards her?' Sir Charles says.

'Of course I did, I've already said that, but I'm her therapist. Just because I think something doesn't mean I'm going to act on it. It's just not important.'

'You're counselling a beautiful young woman. You've just finished telling us that when she was with you she was like a baby. And then you say it's not important whether you had sexual feelings towards her.'

'No, it's not important because it's just a feeling. I can't control what feelings happen to me. I can only control how I respond. And with a client, I respond by staying in charge. If you understood my profession, you'd understand what I'm talking about. Talk to other therapists. They'll tell you. I'm not some sexual monster.'

Kit starts. 'Gareth, did you ever get a sense that Jane was sexually attracted to you?'

'Yes, this sometimes happens, especially where there's a history of child abuse. I'll admit I was surprised when Jane started coming on. I can usually predict within broad terms the direction of the client's work. When she started flirting, I dealt with it as best I could.'

'How did you feel?'

'My job as therapist is to stay in charge and I did.'

'How did you respond?'

'At first, I tried to ignore it and respond to Jane's other needs, then I tried confrontation which wound us up in black silence. Then I tried responding, not sexually, but responding to the sexual coming on with caring. Jane's sense of her self was less solid than I thought.

'Progress was slow and nothing lasting seemed to be happening. Jane had two ways of being—black with anger or promiscuous. In the course of therapy, she had one or two psychotic episodes.'

Kit pushes. 'If you didn't have sex and Jane's not lying, then one of you must be mistaken. Which one?'

'Jane's a very disturbed young woman. Maybe she even believes I did seduce her.'

'Can you think of any reason Victim B and Victim C would lie about you?' These are the as yet unnamed women providing supporting statements in the court case.

'The other two clients don't say I seduced them. One says I talked about sex. She also says she came to see me because she was having sexual difficulties. Of course I'd talk about sex. The other client, Victim B, I don't know who she is. I have no record of anyone even vaguely similar to the case she presents.'

'What problems have you had with clients in the past?'

'The same as every therapist,' Gareth smiles. 'I don't always do as well as I'd like, some clients do better than others.'

'The Psychologists' Registration Board is investigating you as well. What do they think?'

'You'd have to ask them.'

Kit asks whether Gareth thinks he did anything wrong in Jane's therapy. He smiles. 'Where do I start? Obviously, I've been over and over my case notes since this happened. I think I got something wrong in the transference. I started feeling frustrated when Jane wouldn't work, I wanted more for her than she wanted. I pushed. My notes reflect this.'

'Did you discuss this with a counselling supervisor?'

'I haven't found someone in Melbourne I'd be happy working with yet.'

It goes on and on. Kit glares, pieces of Gareth's hair spring out and fall onto his forehead, he shifts around in his seat, he looks uncomfortable which is what Kit wants. He looks unfinished. He looks guilty.

I ask whether he knows any reason Jane Kidman might say this happened if it didn't. 'It's as I've already said, sometimes clients get very mixed up in therapy. We're talking about someone in distress, who needs professional help, but who can turn on the one person who can help them.'

'Are you saying she's doing this to get you back?'

'I don't know. I can't know. But I've thought about it. Jane became very attached to me, she used to call me at home, write me letters. It's quite normal for someone with Jane's background to idealise a therapist. Maybe she felt rejected when I terminated therapy, became enraged. There are certain personality disorders that could lead to that kind of behaviour. Borderlines, for instance, present a very similar structure to Jane. Maybe I underestimated the extent of damage to her sense of self.'

Kit says, 'Why did you decide to terminate therapy?'

Gareth takes too long to answer. 'I didn't think things were proceeding well. I felt I was getting too involved with her, caring too much when she didn't work, worrying about her. I decided it would be best to terminate. I thought that eventually, if I kept seeing her, I'd respond emotionally to her.' There's another ripple of movement in the bodies along the table, it's like symbiosis, as if they've merged into one organism. 'So I let her go. It wasn't an easy decision, it never is. With hindsight, it was probably a bad decision. But that's what I did. I gave Jane the name of a psychiatrist specialising in abuse, advised her strongly to take up that option, and let her go.'

'Gareth', Kit says, 'you're saying that in your treatment of Jane Kidman, you found yourself becoming invested, you got slack about time and money, you don't have a supervisor. You'd have to agree you were vulnerable to further breaches of ethics.'

'I know what you're saying. I didn't follow the rules. Yes, these are breaches in the most literal sense. But I know what I'm doing. And I know whose interests I have at heart. I would never take advantage of a client. Never.' Gareth holds his head in his hands, wipes his eyes with both palms, looks back up at Kit. She asks whether he has any regrets about the way he dealt with Jane Kidman. 'Only that I wish I hadn't terminated. I think it was a mistake. I should have worked through my own issues and helped Jane. I'm sure I could have.' He pushes his hair back off his face, wipes his eyes again, looks down at his hands in his lap.

At the end of the day of interviews I feel muddled and exhausted. The written evidence before the committee includes Jane Kidman's allegation and Gareth's response supported by statements from eminent academics, practising psychotherapists and therapy associations from all over Australia. Daniel contacted the vice-chancellor of Gareth's former university who said that they were sorry to lose him. We talked with his current boss and three colleagues. We met two female students who'd been his clients, picked at random. They both said he'd helped them, one of them knew about the case. The staff couldn't have been more supportive. One colleague said he'd been a great addition to their team, he'd helped her, he'd built up a solid reputation in a short time. One of them cried, said she'd couldn't believe this could happen. She told us about Gareth's little girl. She said his wife had abandoned her, Gareth was a wonderful man and a wonderful parent. She told us this was a travesty of justice. She was a large woman with magenta on her lips. She was like this extra energy in the room I didn't need.

Sir Charles suggests we leave detailed discussion until our next meeting, after Kit and I have spoken with Jane Kidman. The union nominees walk out together, silent, unreadable. Kit won't be drawn into conversation either. All she says is that institutions are hopeless at handling difficult cases. Her eyes move all over the place as she says it.

# TWENTY-THREE

John spends the afternoon ambling in and out of my office while I go through my in-tray like a robot. I watch the edge of a piece of letterhead against my desk, it blends into the wood. Then I'm walking up the back stairs at Uncle Jack's, slowly, avoiding pieces of sunlight. He's building a new kitchen, his hammer stops when Auntie Clare speaks. 'Maybe you'd better tell them.'

'Clare, it's up to them.'

'At least you could tell them she's asking.'

'They know that.'

'It's wrong.'

Back in my office, I can't believe the things people ask me. The Student Administration people want to know whether orange is an acceptable hood colour for a new postgraduate award in Health since orange is a colour already used by Arts. I reply no on the basis that nothing further will come back to me about it. Sometimes I worry that a decision I make will actually affect someone's life.

I leave late and feel a rush of cold when I get out of the lift to the low yellow lights and large shadows of the carpark. I think of Gareth Ford and his Mercedes Benz. I start towards my car then go back to the lift, press the call button. The number 4 lights up, then 5, 4, 3, 2, 1, G, LG. The doors open and a clerk from Finance emerges, she's carrying a folder, she makes a joke about me being early for work, I say I forgot something. I get in the lift and go up to the ground floor to

Campus Administration. The offices are closed now, there's only the tiny rectangular green exit lights to guide me through. I have a master key, it's so quiet here, not even the low level noise of computers and air-conditioners to soothe the world. I go through the cashier's office, the enquiries counter, through another area that I don't know the name of, to Counselling. I stand in the waiting area for a few minutes, let my eyes adjust to the darkness, walk down a long corridor, see his door among doors. It's not locked. If I see anyone, I'll say I was looking for something. It's not really a lie.

Gareth Ford's office is on the non-river side of the building. It must look over a small concrete courtyard. I switch on the light, blind myself, readjust. There's a small desk in one corner, a picture frame covered in pink and blue shells with a photo of Gareth's daughter Hilary as a smiling toddler, a blotter, what looks like a diary. Above the desk on the wall are three or four small-fingered finger paintings on butcher's paper. I go to the desk, flick through the diary which is full of small neat handwriting of notes, diagrams and names. I read a couple of entries. Peter mother d 2, father ?? VPR with a circle around the R. Partner Mandy scared? I don't know who I am anymore underlined in quotes. 4 pm Simone. I don't want to talk today exclamation mark. Weekly. There's a drawing then, three circles, overlapping. I think of the Venn diagram and year four maths. It's this year's diary and I don't find any entries for Jane Kidman. I put the diary back.

I go through the desk drawers. They're messy, pencils, pens, erasers, thumb tacks spilled, paper clips, a stapler, bits of paper with notes and drawings that look like they've been shoved in there in a hurry. There's a picture of Gareth in the bottom drawer, holding Hilary, standing next to a short fat woman, must be his wife. Hilary's smiling, pulling Gareth's beard. He's looking at her and away from his wife, his mouth open, poking a face. They're at the beach, you can see the water behind, he's not wearing a shirt, the arm around his daughter looks strong. He's wearing long shorts and a checked baseball cap. It's a good photo although I think the horizon's crooked.

In the middle of the room there are three chairs around a coffee table. A blank whiteboard leans against the wall behind one of the chairs. There's a box of tissues and an ashtray full of butts on the table. They're not supposed to smoke in their offices. I try to imagine Gareth Ford in here with someone. I sit in the different chairs, I thought I'd feel spooky, but I don't. I feel sort of safe. Behind a small couch there's a mattress standing on its side. What am I looking for?

A bookcase near the desk is filled with books like *Why am I afraid to be?*, *Coming home*, *Human sexuality*. I flick through one or two of his books, filled with pen marks, highlighting. I find a small blue envelope. The door opens.

'Miss Lanois.'

It's one of our security guards. 'Ray,' I say. 'How are you?'

'Good. Yourself?'

'Fine,' I say.

'You lost?' A wily old smile like he knows something.

'I came in here to find someone and noticed the light on. I got interested in this.' I hold up a book, I think I'm smart to think so quickly on my feet. I look at the book again, it's called *The female orgasm*. I put it back on the shelf quickly. 'Anyway Ray,' I'm blushing. 'Good to see you again.' I wonder who he'll tell.

At home, I open the envelope I took from Gareth Ford's office. Inside there's a card.

I need to see you. Call me
today. Please.
Love,
Jane

It's the sort of note you write to someone you know really well, someone you can keep it really short with. This isn't the sort of writing I imagine from a client to a therapist.

# TWENTY-FOUR

Jane Kidman is only twenty but she looks much younger than I expected. She's small and slight with fair skin and bright red hair. Her ears are pierced in too many places to count, right up in the cartilage part. She wears oversized black jeans, a tight white T-shirt and a coloured vest. She has this expensive street kid look that says fuck you in a refined way. She tilts her head when she sits down and screws one side of her nose up like Elvis Presley.

'Jane, I really appreciate your willingness to talk to us,' I say.

Jane doesn't say anything.

Kit is gentle, she talks about how difficult it is sometimes to know what people's approaches mean. She talks about responsibility, the responsibility staff have to students, the responsibility students have for their own lives. She talks about Jane's allegations but not as if they're true necessarily. I'm surprised by her evenness.

'Jane,' I say, 'Gareth Ford denies the allegations you've made. He says he did a lot of regressive work with you and it would be easy to misunderstand his intentions. What do you think about that?'

'Unless they've started doing regressive work with their dicks, I'd say he's lying.' She's smiling. Her voice is low and confident but I get an impression it's not a very thick layer. She looks at the closed door. She hasn't looked at Kit or me since she sat down. She folds her arms, sits so low in her chair I think she'll slip onto the floor.

'Your written allegations stand then, that Gareth Ford initiated and developed a sexual relationship with you.'

'Yep.'

'Is there anything you want to tell us in addition to what you've already said in your allegations?'

She sits up again, looks away, takes in a huge breath, blows out through nearly closed lips. She rubs her eye. I notice her index finger is pink and raw where she's bitten the nail. 'My doctor said I shouldn't have come here.' There's a long pause. 'I get mixed up.' Another pause. 'I'm thinking maybe I'm mixed up, you know?' She looks up at me then. Her eyes are green. There are traces of freckles on her face.

'No, I'm not sure I do know Jane. Are you saying you might be mixed up about what happened with Gareth Ford?'

'No,' she says quickly. Then she laughs, a sort of snort. 'Yes, that's what I'm saying. Maybe I'm mixed up. Sometimes I'm not sure about what I remember. My doctor says I shouldn't talk to you.' She presses her palms against her eyes.

'Are you saying maybe things happened differently from how you thought they did?'

'Yes.' She shifts in her seat, takes in another big breath, and out, looks relieved. 'I don't know what I'm saying.'

She won't talk after that. She looks at her hands in her lap. We stay for a while, ask questions, offer to adjourn, offer to write things down. Offer to have a little break, offer coffee. Eventually, she looks up again. 'I guess my doctor was right. My letter stands.' She smiles, stands up quickly and walks out the door which she leaves open behind her.

# TWENTY-FIVE

The misconduct committee meets in the small stuffy conference room on the fifth level of the Chancellery Building, five
of us sitting forward under fluorescent lights, our dirty glasses
and coffee cups scattered over the other end of the too small
table.

We start with a simple question. Is a sexual relationship
with a student misconduct within the meaning of by-law
number seven if it happens in a staff member's private practice? The legal advice says it is. Misconduct includes any act
that damages the university, sex with a student could damage
the university and could therefore be regarded as misconduct.
We argue it out for five hours. Staff rep Harry Gutterl says
private practice has nothing to do with the university, Diana
McGarry says it's not relevant because Gareth Ford didn't
have sex with Jane Kidman, Kit argues for a new by-law that
includes sexual misconduct, I quote and requote the legal
advice, tell them it's simple, read from the by-law, start again.

The committee finally agrees that if a student counsellor
has a sexual relationship with a student, it damages the
university, it's misconduct, even if it occurs in private practice.
At 9.30 pm, we order pizzas, break for quarter of an hour,
resume.

There are dark rings under all ten eyes around the table.
Sir Charles says, 'She's a child, eighteen when this happened.'
He has daughters. His spectacles slip along his nose.

Harry Gutterl agrees, I think he's religious. 'I think it's

obvious they had sex. Maybe she consented, I don't know, we'll never know that. But I think they had sex. And we've already decided that's misconduct.'

Diana McGarry disagrees. 'We've been over all of this before. We know what Gareth's like, we've seen the letters people have written, the things people say about him. And we know Jane is a student with a great imagination. It's obvious.'

Kit says the only thing that's obvious is the damage to Jane Kidman. 'We must give the complainant the benefit of the doubt. She's had the courage to come forward, no one does that falsely, she's made a complaint, we have to respond.'

Sir Charles starts again. 'Maybe we need to have a straw poll, just see where people might vote at this stage. Do we think we might be ready for that?'

We finish at 2 am. At 7.30, I'm back at work with Daniel and Bill in Daniel's office. 'The last straw poll was three to two guilty. Kit and Harry Gutterl were guilty right up to the end. But Sir Charles changed his mind at the last minute, argued guilty all night, then suddenly agreed with me we didn't have the evidence. So it was three to two not guilty.'

'You'd expect Charles to go for not guilty,' Bill says. 'Maybe he was taking a line.' He smiles.

'What do you mean?' I say.

He looks at Daniel. 'Strategy,' he says. 'If you take a particular view strongly enough, people automatically slide towards the opposite view. Human nature. And Sir Charles was never going to find Ford guilty.'

'Why not?'

Bill looks at Daniel again, tilts his head, Daniel nods. 'You wouldn't remember. Early seventies. Well-known Melbourne obstetrician alleged to have interfered with a female patient.' He pauses, rubs his hands together. 'It was Charles. He got off, remade himself, now he's a pillar.'

'I didn't know that. Did he do it?'

'Never went to court,' Bill says. 'It was only rumours really.'

'Of course he didn't,' Daniel says. 'Can you imagine him doing something like that?'

I think about this and I have no idea. 'I wish someone had told me this before.'

'It's nothing to do with this case,' Daniel says. 'It was twenty years ago and it settled. Nothing's happened since.'

'I guess you're right.' I still feel uneasy. 'It might have been better to have a different council member on the committee though. Do other people know about this?'

'I doubt it,' Bill says. 'Too long ago.'

At the end of the meeting, Daniel asks me for five minutes. His hands are in his pockets. 'You did a great job Adele. Once council's over, assuming they agree with the recommendation, we can concentrate on the court case. And we're going to win, I can feel it.'

# TWENTY-SIX

Last night I set the mousetrap again then dreamed they'd taken over my flat. I wandered through a moving grey carpet, soft and warm under my feet, to get to the kitchen. This morning the pumpkin seed has gone, the trap is sprung but there's no dead mouse. I feel relieved.

I make notes on the Gareth Ford submission to university council, practise my introduction in the mirror in my bedroom as I'm getting ready for work. 'This submission relates to an allegation blah blah blah . . . Mr Ford became intimately involved with a student, blah blah blah.' I kiss the mirror when I say intimately. I poke my tongue, open my eyes wide, look crazy at the mirror. Am I crazy?

The chancellor sits at one end of the room in a chair that's bigger than the others. Behind him is a portrait of Sir James Walters. I'm the secretary so I sit on the chancellor's left. Daniel sits opposite me, on the chancellor's right. The 20 council members—externals, government appointments and elected staff, students and graduates—sit around the table, in the same place as last time.

I'm nervous with the energy in the room and not ready for discussion about Gareth Ford. Sir Charles is talking to me. He looks like my father who I see moving towards me slowly from the other side of the room. 'Don't you get it love? Let's try another way.' My exercise book filled with his blue pen, the marks go through two or three pages. My school uniform getting too short. I'm growing too quickly. 'Look at me when I'm talking to you Adele. Don't you understand anything?'

Sir Charles is smiling to reassure me, but it's not working. I've done my introduction, I can feel my heart going thump in my head, my voice comes out in sharp little waves. I can feel my neck hot in patches. I've missed something. A staff member on council speaks, a professor from the Arts faculty, Jim Hickson. 'Reading these papers I find it impossible to accept the committee's finding. Is Mr Ford available to talk to us?' The 25 faces around the table are looking at me. Behind them the walls are covered with portraits of former vice-chancellors and chancellors. No one is smiling. I wish we'd had time to talk about this in the pre-council breakfast this morning. But Daniel was late and we got caught up on something else.

'Through you chancellor, yes I'm sure he would be Professor Hickson,' I say. Daniel frowns. 'If that's the way council wishes to proceed. Perhaps I wasn't clear. The misconduct committee has given every opportunity for those involved to be heard. We collected verbal evidence and all relevant submissions. On the balance of evidence, the committee is recommending Mr Ford be found not guilty.'

'I appreciate that,' Jim Hickson says. 'But I'm being asked to vote on this issue on the basis of what's before me which is a serious allegation, a staff member's response and the committee's submission.' There are nods around the table. 'I think I need more to make up my mind.'

Daniel says, 'Council set up a misconduct committee to carry out an investigation on its behalf. The committee carried out its investigation and found no evidence of misconduct. I can't see how we can argue with that.'

'How do we know he's innocent?' Jim Hickson says.

'The committee's not saying he's innocent,' Daniel says. 'They're saying there's no evidence he's guilty. Frankly, I think we've got no choice.'

Sir Charles says, 'This was a difficult case, a student making serious claims in relation to a staff member. I chaired this committee and strongly support the recommendation.' He sniffs. 'Having said that, I've also spoken privately with the vice-chancellor about action to monitor the staff member's activities more closely in future.' This is news to me. If he's not guilty, why are we monitoring anything? I must ask Daniel about this.

Council approves the misconduct committee's recommendations, that Gareth Ford be found not guilty of misconduct and that Jane Kidman be offered counselling through the equity section. The vote is nine to seven with four abstentions and could easily have gone another way.

'I'm glad that's over,' I say to Bill on the way back to the chancellery. 'For a while there, I thought things were going against us.' Bill doesn't say anything, looks preoccupied, he was quiet in council too.

As we're waiting for the lift, he says, 'How confident are you that you're right?'

'As sure as I can be. You've read the documents. What do you think?'

'That's just it. On the evidence, I can't get to your conclusion.' Daniel comes up behind us and tells me to call Gareth.

'Maybe I'd better do that,' Bill says.

'It's Adele's win,' Daniel says. We get into the lift together. Daniel's carrying his council papers in one arm, he touches my arm with the other. 'And she's got a soft spot for our counsellor.' Bill doesn't respond.

Back in my office on the phone, Gareth wants to know when he can come back to work. 'Next week.' He says he's grateful for my support. 'It was council's decision,' I say. 'And it's not over yet. I'll set up a meeting with the lawyers.'

# TWENTY-SEVEN

Jef Blackwell was right about one thing. We've had press. Daniel issues statements, won't be interviewed. Our public affairs director smiles weakly and tells me there's no such thing as bad publicity. Bill doesn't say much to me when we pass in the corridor, withdraws from the case, leaves it to Daniel who leaves it to me.

Despite our lack of comment, the press construct Jane Kidman. She's not from a wealthy family, she's never been in trouble. She's an ordinary kid from an ordinary family who went to seek help with her studies. She's a bright kid, a good kid, the sort of kid every parent wants. A well-balanced, happy kid. And then she met a monster.

They don't use her name but they publish a description, mention her distinguished academic record, details of her allegations of sex. I wonder where they get the information. I send a memo round to managers about confidentiality.

We get a call from a national women's magazine that's going to run a feature. I tell Daniel he should be interviewed. He agrees but says I'm doing a great job and it's better for a woman to handle inquiries. I wonder about this. In the end they don't interview anyone, they just quote our statement, do a much bigger story on sex and therapy, include the picture of Gareth eating a hamburger.

Mark Campinelli tells me there are calls coming in, from students, from parents, from staff. I get letters, crazy letters, telling me Gareth Ford should be castrated, telling me the university is blind, deaf and dumb, telling me it's a women's issue, telling me I'm letting down all women everywhere (this from one of my own staff).

Daniel says we knew it was going to be rough. I slide through days as if I'm not there. At home in bed, I dream that Jane Kidman turns up in all the wrong places wanting to hurt me.

# TWENTY-EIGHT

Uncle Jack said Daddy put the car in neutral and put on the handbrake. He said it to comfort us, to show Daddy was in charge right to the end. I keep thinking of this. I have this image of him at the beach in his brown swimming trunks with a yellow stripe down one side, the hair on his chest, his soft white stomach and hips. I imagine him in the carport with his shirt off, not moving, his pink belly turning grey then blue. For some reason, I feel angry. I can't get used to the idea that he's no longer breathing.

I took photographs at the funeral. There's one of Uncle Jack holding Mummy around the middle as if she's a little girl he's carrying, Auntie Clare lost and grey behind them. Daddy's brother, Michel, from France. He left the day after the funeral. Bill Pozzi, smiling, saying everything would be all right.

I took a day off work. Now I'm back and papers move from my in-tray to my out-tray with a soft thud. People avoid me. I feel frustrated but I can't quite put my finger on it. There are cards. Jef Blackwell. I'm so sorry to know of your loss with silver embossed deepest sympathy. When we talk on the telephone, he doesn't mention it. He says we're briefing Malcolm Hughes. He's one of Daddy's favourite barristers. 'I had another look at the statements last night,' I say. 'Especially the one from the second client, Victim B, very different from Victim C.' Victims B and C are the authors of the two supporting statements listed in evidence in the legal case. 'Victim C says he put his hand on her leg. He asked her about her sex life. But Victim B says he had sex with her. Outside therapy but sex all the same. I'm wondering why she'd do that.'

'Bear in mind the case we're defending,' Jef says. 'The claim is negligence, we knew about him, we did nothing. It's not whether he had sex, it's whether we knew.'

'I don't particularly want to get off on a technicality Jef. If he did what Jane Kidman said, I think we'd settle, pay whatever's fair. But I think he's innocent and I think we can prove it.'

'Of course. And the statements from the other women are weak at any rate. Victim B says she voluntarily consented to a sexual relationship a long time after therapy finished. It wasn't anything to do with therapy. She's making no claim against him. Hopefully, it won't even be admitted. We'll argue that the claims he had other relationships have nothing to do with whether he had this relationship.'

He's making this up as he goes along and I'm not satisfied. 'We need to find out if there's a link between Jane Kidman and Victim B. Can you put someone on it?'

'No problem. As soon as we know a name.'

Emily drops over at home with cinnamon loaf and brandy. 'You're not returning my calls,' she says.

'I haven't felt like company.' She's down the hallway before I can say I still don't. But she gets me talking. 'I want to spend more time with Mummy.'

'What about you?' she says. 'How are you feeling?'

I swallow. 'I went down to the beach on the weekend after I got home. I watched the water, didn't even go for a walk. Know what I felt?' She doesn't. 'This terrible sense of longing. Not sad. Longing. It's an awful feeling.'

Emily asks me what I want. I tell her I want to look after Mummy. She asks again. 'What about for you, Adele, what do you want just for yourself?'

'I don't know,' I say. 'That's the funniest thing Em. If I try to think about what I want for me, I come up with a blank.'

# TWENTY-NINE

I arrive at the hotel at 7.30 am, walk through the largest foyer in the world up a *Gone with the Wind* staircase to a huge display of dried flowers on a marble table. Jef Blackwell and Malcolm Hughes are waiting on either end of a couch. They stand when I approach, they make a pair in their black suits.

Malcolm Hughes has well receded curly silver hair, blue eyes, a bit of a tummy and a smile that's just for me. 'Adele, so nice to see you again.'

We go to a private dining room without windows. A waiter stands over me until I realise I'm holding on to my napkin which he wants to spread on my lap. I apologise. He says Madam. Everything's muffled by thick carpet and wallpaper and air-conditioning.

'How's your father enjoying his retirement?' Malcolm refuses orange juice and points to the teapot.

Jef looks horrified. 'He died,' I say. 'A week ago. I thought you knew.'

Malcolm's face freezes. 'Adele, I'm so sorry. No I didn't know. I've been abroad.'

'Please, don't worry about it. Heart attack.' I take a breadroll from the silver basket in the middle of the table.

Gareth arrives with his solicitor, Mary McGrath, who I've only spoken to on the phone. She has a suntan, hazel eyes and a rich voice like someone on radio. She wears a beige suit. We introduce ourselves. A boy with black hair brings more coffee. Cereals and toast. A hot breakfast. Jef gives a rundown on the case, affidavits, evidence. Mary stops him, clarifies, questions. She's on top of things. We talk about likely scenarios. Malcolm says very little, watches Gareth who looks relaxed. More coffee. Malcolm starts. Slowly at first, he asks Gareth questions about Jane Kidman. What they did, how they did it, what happened. He gets faster, nastier. Gareth's too sure. I get the impression Malcolm doesn't like him.

I walk out with Gareth and Mary. 'How'd I do?' Gareth says.

'He took a lot of notes,' I say.

'Is that a bad sign?'

'I'm about to find out.'

'He needs to work Adele,' Malcolm says when I get back to the dining room. 'I felt better before I talked to him.'

'He's probably telling the truth. That has to count for something.'

Malcolm looks at me, doesn't respond straight away. 'What jury will accept that he lay on the floor with a girl every week for over a year and didn't become sexually involved? We need to work on that.'

'He has a terrific reputation. Colleagues speak highly of him. He's really helped some kids, in his own time. You should see the letters we've got.' Malcolm looks at me and raises an eyebrow, it's one of those Are you all right? looks— the sort Bill Pozzi gives me in meetings. 'From other therapists, students, parents, therapy associations. They all say he does a tremendous job.'

'That's the line we need to push, a good man doing a tremendous service for the community victimised by a woman with problems about men. Something like that anyway. It's a pity we're unable to use the girl's false claim.' He taps the table a few times with a teaspoon, puts it back in place. 'Maybe we can use it without using it. Have you mentioned it to the other side?'

'Not yet,' Jef says.

'Give them a whiff, hint we've got something we can use. Might make them more reasonable.'

'What about the statements from the other two women?' I

say. 'Victims B and C. Jef thinks their evidence won't be admitted.'

'Possibly,' Malcolm says. 'We'll argue that a claim he had sex with another client is irrelevant to whether he had sex with this client.'

'They'll argue a former sexual relationship establishes a predisposition,' I say.

'Of course they will,' Malcolm smiles. 'And I'd be willing to put my money with them. We need their names Jef, something on them. Establish they might be lying too.'

'We've asked,' Jef says. 'They're holding out, arguing for suppression.' He looks at Malcolm, gives another rundown on the case, more realistic now with Gareth gone. 'The case against us looks stronger than we thought. We feel Kidman will be a strong witness. If we can't find a way to use the confidential material about her earlier complaint, she'll be even stronger. If Victim B's evidence is allowed, it weakens our case. I've talked informally with the other side. They're confident. And we've got the wrong judge,' he says. 'They're paranoid about women's rights because of the bad press lately. A few are very sensitive, ours is one of them.'

'They still don't want a settlement?' I say.

Jef looks at Malcolm again. 'My intelligence is that they want this trial. They say they want to expose Gareth Ford.'

Back at work, I'm sitting at the coffee table in my office playing with a fountain pen I bought on the weekend. It's about eight inches long, a maroon base with gold diamantes glued all over it. It's very special. I roll it between my thumb and index finger, watch the diamantes catch pieces of light. John watches me from the outer office, watches me watching my diamante pen. The lawyers don't believe Gareth Ford, they believe Jane Kidman. And I think my secretary thinks I've gone over the edge.

The phone rings and I watch, phones don't move when they ring. 'Adele, you want to pick that up?' John is looking at me. I ask who it is. 'Gareth Ford,' he says. He gets up and closes the door into my office.

'How'd I do?' Gareth says.

'They think we've got some work to do, but they're pretty confident.' I talk about evidence and the way it emerges over time, becomes solid, polished. 'You start with an idea and build from there.'

'So it didn't go too well?' I think he's smiling. I say it could have been better. 'I don't think your lawyers understood regression therapy very well.'

I agree. 'Malcolm Hughes was worried about that. So was I to be honest.'

'I have to tell the truth.'

'Truth's largely the slant you put on it.' He says I'm talking in a nice way about lying. And I guess I am. He says he doesn't really care anymore. He says he wants it to be over. I notice John is still watching me through the glass wall. 'Do you think my secretary's a bit strange?' I say.

'I don't know,' Gareth says.

'It's just that he spends his whole day staring at me lately. As if I've done something terrible to him.'

Gareth thinks this is funny, says it tells us more about my secretary than it tells us about me. Then he asks me to dinner. 'You can tell me what I should say in court.'

# THIRTY

There are long pauses at home, that's the only tangible difference, spaces that would have been filled by Daddy's grouchy voice.

We're eating dinner, fish I bought on the beach, baby carrots, microwaved potatoes. Mummy doesn't look after herself, I'm sure she doesn't get up during the day unless I'm here. Uncle Jack avoids my questions. I want to pack her in my suitcase and take her back to Melbourne. She's so tiny, almost nothing. 'What's this one?' she says. I tell her it's snapper. 'It's nice.'

'I thought we could go to the markets tomorrow.' She says that would be nice.

I drive south along the ocean road and watch waves hurl themselves against rocks a long way below. It's a blustery day with hard cold rain. I stop at the bakery at Apollo Bay and buy two fairy cakes with pink icing and hundreds and thousands. Then I head inland to Melbourne.

Emily calls, she's got night duty. 'What are you doing for dinner?'

'Running late.'

'Who?'

'Remember that counsellor I told you about? We're meeting to talk about the case.'

'I thought he got off.'

'He was found not guilty in the university. There's still a legal case.'

'Was he in *The Age* during the week?'

'Yeah, the papers are pretty interested.'

'I didn't realise it was the same case, the guy in the paper looked like evil incarnate.'

'That's just the way they portray him Em.'

Gareth arrives early and waits for me in the sitting room. I put on a long floppy dress, watch russet and gold stripes of cotton surround me. I feel rich.

'Is this you and your mother?' He's holding a photo of me as a little girl. I'm in a white frock, big dark curls, my mother just behind me to the left, her jaw dominating. I say yes. 'You were really beautiful.' He picks up another photo, me as a teenager, towering over my small, slim mother and almost as tall as my father. 'You don't look much like your parents, do you?'

'I take after my father's family.'

'Adolescence, who'd go through it again?' He turns to me and smiles. 'You look wonderful.'

We take his car, the Mercedes I saw in the Walters carpark the night he frightened me. I look across at him, I find it hard to understand how I can feel so differently. He drives slowly as if he's not interested in getting anywhere. We go to a restaurant he knows, two-storeys on the bay looking over St Kilda beach. Inside there are polished floors and waiters in long aprons. We sit near a fire. Outside the bay is black.

I talk to him about his evidence, suggest he needs to think about how a non-specialist might view him. 'You have to think about this from a more general point of view.'

'Why? Don't you think people will understand?'

'No I don't.'

'My sort of therapy is more common than you realise. You'd be surprised how many people would be familiar with my work.'

'Perhaps.' I think of Emily lying on the floor with her therapist. Emily has five brothers and no sisters, she grew up on a sheep property in the Goulburn Valley, she was expelled from her local school and I can't imagine she'd lie on the floor for anyone unless she wanted to. 'It's not so much when you talk about therapy as when you talk about your own sexual feelings. It gets harder to put together that nothing happened. From one point of view,' I add.

'I have to tell the truth or I'm finished.' He says he doesn't trust the lawyers. 'There's nothing wrong with my work. I help people. Which is more than they do.' A waiter arrives, I order oysters followed by grilled yellowfin tuna and sweet potato. Gareth orders the same and some wine.

He pushes his glasses up his nose. 'But I'm glad you brought it up,' he says. 'I've been wanting to talk to you.' He looks out at the black water then back at me, brings his joined palms up to his lips as if praying. 'I've been thinking about Jane, going over my case notes. I keep asking myself whether there was anything I did. I know I had transference problems. Maybe what happened is partly my fault.'

'What do you mean?'

'Why would she do this if I didn't get something wrong? Send some signal? I've been over and over it in my head, maybe there was something, I don't know.' He slumps in his chair and looks straight in front.

'She lied before.' He looks at me, breathes in as if he's going to say something but doesn't. 'It's black and white. You either had sex with her or you didn't Gareth.' He looks at me. 'And you didn't. That's what matters. Her reasons aren't your problem. Maybe she wants money.'

'She's not like that.'

'You said yourself she's very disturbed, she's angry with you about the way you finished therapy.'

He pauses and looks out to the water. 'I just feel bad. This isn't what I wanted to happen. No matter what, the outcome's awful. Jane's not well, she needs help. If she wins, that's going to destroy me and her. If she loses, what will that do to her?' He considers this question. I say Jane's behaviour tells us more about Jane than it tells us about Gareth. He smiles. 'You've been fantastic you know. I couldn't have got through this without your help.'

Food arrives and I use the opportunity to change the subject. I ask him about being back at work. 'Max has been great, he's put me on long-term work. I'm not very interested in quick fix stuff, assertiveness and whiteboards. I'm much more interested in what really motivates people.' He drinks wine. 'Like you.' He smiles. 'What motivates you.'

'And what's your conclusion?'

'You'd have to come to my office for an assessment.'

'Right,' I say. 'For only $99.'

'For you,' he says, '$89.'

# THIRTY-ONE

'Someone's got to ring him,' Jef Blackwell sounds agitated on the other end of the phone. 'I can't believe it. How am I going to tell Malcolm?' 'You know what this looks like, don't you?'

'Have you got a copy?'

'No, I got a call from Kidman's solicitor. Guess what your therapist did, he said. But I didn't know. Ford didn't tell me. He didn't even tell his own solicitor.'

When Gareth calls back it's after five. 'What are you still doing there at this time?' he says.

'Gareth, did you write to Jane Kidman?'

'How did you know?'

'Her solicitors have been in touch to let our solicitors know. It's courtesy.'

'I thought it might help.' He says he'll drop around a copy of the letter to me at home. I tell him I'll be there by eight.

He arrives with Hilary, I show them into the sitting room. Gareth looks at my pewter cabinet while Hilary holds onto his right leg. I read the letter.

Jane,

I think I can help you. I can understand why you've done and said what you've done and said. I know how difficult your issues are, how frightening that stuff can be. I know my decision to stop therapy was difficult for

you. I think in retrospect I should have worked with you
for longer before finishing.

I just want you to know I'm still here if you need
help.

Gareth

When I look up, he's smiling at me, as if he wants me to tell
him what a good job he's done. I want to yell at him. His
hair's a mess. His shirt looks like it was ironed a long time
ago. 'Gareth, this wasn't a good idea.'

'Why? If Jane came for one session, we could work this
through. She'd be back on her feet and I'd be out of this crazy
situation.'

'This looks like someone who's guilty and trying to fix it.'

'What do you mean?'

'Telling her you got it wrong. Gareth, this is very bad.'

He doesn't get it. 'I just wrote her a letter. I know her really
well. I know she's doing this but I don't really believe she
wants to get me. She's just angry at the world. She needs
help.'

I offer him coffee. He looks around when we go to the
kitchen. I notice the sprung mousetrap in the middle of the
floor, no pumpkin seed, no mouse. He says he didn't realise
his letter would cause so much trouble. He doesn't seem
particularly bothered about it. Hilary hides and he pretends
to be looking for her. He uses this sing-song voice, 'Do you
know where Hilary is Adele? Is she . . . in the pantry? No,
she's not in the pantry.' He tries two or three more places,
says, 'I think she's . . . under the table,' at which point he
grabs her under the table, says, 'Now I've got you, I'm going
to . . . kiss you on the tummy.' She giggles, thinks this is great,
gets him to play over and over again while I wonder how
we're ever going to get through the court case.

# THIRTY-TWO

When the doorbell rings at 6 am I figure it's Emily on the way home from work. I go out in my dressing gown. It's Jane Kidman.

She's wearing denim jeans and an orange shirt. Her eyes are all over the place and she doesn't seem to be focusing. Maybe she's drugged. 'I want to talk again,' she says. She looks towards the backyard where Miss Bartlett is hanging washing. I feel nervous.

'Do you want me to set up another meeting?'

'No, I just want to talk to you, away from uni.'

'Come in then.' I take her through to the sitting room. We sit down near the heater, Jane sits in my satellite-dish chair so I have to sit on the couch.

'I feel tired all the time,' she says. I'm just about to say, So do I, when I remember who she is. 'I've come to say what happened with Gareth.' There's a long pause where she looks at the carpet. 'In the first session, he threw a cushion towards me and told me to grab the corner. He started pulling me towards him, I pulled too. He said everybody wants something. I didn't get it.

'I really liked him though, right from the first session. He was fun and interested in me.' She snorts. 'I'd never been for counselling before so I didn't know what it would be like.' This is a lie. Her student file has letters from a psychiatrist to explain a long absence in first year. 'My marks were going down, I was just starting second year, and I'd done great in

124

first. I was missing Keith, my boyfriend, we'd split up. Gareth said I had to trust him and that when I took some risks I'd feel better. I used to get little, that's what he called it, I'd cry like a baby. We'd lie on a mattress on the floor and he'd curl around behind me. I got more and more depressed and all I wanted to do was see him. He was like my lifeline, the only thing that helped me face the scary things I had to face. I still think that, he was my lifeline, he helped me a lot.

'One day, when he was lying behind me on the mattress, I felt his hard dick digging into my bum. I was sure it was a hard dick. I didn't say anything. Some time after that, maybe a month, we were talking, I'd been little, he caressed me, just moved hair out of my face, but I knew it wasn't affection. That's when it started, in the session after that. I thought the best thing in the world was happening to me, I felt really alive.' She smiles for the first time, she looks so young when she smiles, but it's gone quickly. 'Then things didn't go so well. I got more and more down. When we had sex he didn't seem to care about me as much as he did at other times. I got worse and worse but I still wanted him in my life, all the time. I used to ring him. Sometimes he sounded distracted, like he couldn't care less what happened to me.

'We had sex nearly every session. He fixed it up so I'd be the last person for the day and we'd do it in his office. He told me it was wrong what he was doing but he couldn't help himself. He used to get guilty and then talk to me about that. I was pretty mixed up. My marks got better which got Dad off my back but I started wanting to be with Gareth all the time. All the time I was awake I thought about him, things he said, fantasised about the times we'd have. And when I was asleep, I dreamed about him. When he said we couldn't go on seeing each other, I freaked out. I took pills. In the hospital, I saw a lady doctor. Somehow I told her everything, well almost everything. She sent me to another doctor who's my doctor now.

'Sometimes I don't want to go through with this. My doctor says it's part of the healing process. He used me. He abused my trust. It's taken me all this time to just get through. He's got to pay for what he's done.' I get an impression that although it's Jane Kidman talking, she's not real, her face hardly moves, her voice is flat. She's like one of those wind-up dolls with a tape inside.

'Jane, what you've just told me differs from your written statement and I want to check one or two things. Is that okay?'

'What do you mean?'

'Your statement says you didn't actually consent to sex with Gareth Ford.'

'I never said that.'

'So if your statement says that, it's wrong?'

'I never said I didn't consent.'

'And Jane, when we talked at the university, you said you might have been mixed up about more than just whether or not you consented. You said you might have been mixed up about the sex.'

'I get really mixed up sometimes.'

'I know the feeling.'

'Do you? My doctor says there should be a law, she says I should take action. That's what I'm doing.'

I tell her I want to ask some questions about her complaint against Ryan Laing. Kit wouldn't let me raise it in our interview. She blinks a couple of times and looks hard at me. 'What's that got to do with anything?' she says.

'You put in a formal complaint to the equity section that Ryan masturbated in class. Then in interview, you said you could have been mistaken.'

'That's right, we made a mistake.'

'How did you make a mistake? I can't think of much else in a classroom that looks even remotely like an erect penis.'

She smiles. 'Ryan Laing was a little bastard, he did terrible things to girls in the class. We thought that unless there was something bigger than a few dirty pictures, the university wouldn't do anything.'

'So you made it up?'

'Sort of.'

'You sort of made it up?'

'I think he had an erection.'

'Jane, you made a formal complaint about Ryan. He could have been expelled if you'd pursued it.'

'But we didn't, we said we made a mistake.'

'I appreciate that. And last time we met, you told me you thought you might have made a mistake about Gareth Ford.'

'That's true, but it's different. I'm mixed up. Don't you understand that?'

When she leaves, I call Daniel at home. 'What the hell's she visiting you for?' he says.

'What if she's telling the truth?'

'Adele, she's crazy. You saw the expert advice. She's devious and clever. Of course she was convincing. She's got a personality disorder. But you know Gareth. Do you really believe he'd do something like that?'

'I just got a fright, that's all.'

# THIRTY-THREE

John follows me into my office. 'You're late for a meeting in the council chamber and Jef Blackwell called.'

'Call Bill's office and tell them I won't be at the meeting. Where's Jef's number?'

I throw my bag on the floor next to my desk and pushbutton the phone number, cradling the receiver on my shoulder while I power up my computer.

'We hit paydirt,' Jef says. 'Jane Kidman and Victim B.'

'What do you mean?'

'Jane Kidman and Marianne Silvestro, aka Victim B. They see the same psychiatrist. They're mates.' I sit down. I look out the window. For a minute, I can't see the city, I can just see white. Jef's still talking. 'It changes everything. Their whole case is based on independent statements from three women. This implies collusion. It stinks.

'We're calling a meeting with the other side. I talked to her solicitor, Tim Macnamara from Randall and Cross, I told him about Jane Kidman's earlier false complaint as well. He freaked. I think they'll agree to reasonable terms now. Frankly, I don't think Tim knew that the women knew each other. They got Marianne Silvestro's name from the psychiatrist who's seeing both of them. And get this. Silvestro only saw Gareth once. And it was after she and Kidman met. I reckon it's a set up.'

'But why?'

'This psychiatrist they're both seeing is famous for uncovering therapist sexual abuse cases, she's really big on this stuff. Only sometimes, she gets it wrong. We've dug up a number of cases in which she was involved where the plaintiff lost.'

'Do you know the psychiatrist's name?'

'Kaplan.' Hannah Kaplan, the psychiatrist I visited during the misconduct case. She knew Jane Kidman the whole time. Did she have to pretend? Couldn't she have told me? For some reason I feel personally let down by her.

It's not as easy as Jef Blackwell predicted. There's money involved and an agreement that none of us will talk. Gareth is agitated, sitting forward in one of the low blue chairs in my office. 'It's a good settlement,' Jef says. 'We have to pay our costs, the university's up for a bit of money, but they'll drop everything, including any action with the Psychologists' Registration Board. And no publicity.'

Gareth fists one hand into the other open palm a few times, not a gesture I've seen from him before. He looks at the floor and then out the window. 'This feels so weak.'

'Settling doesn't mean you're admitting,' Jef says. 'It just means they agree to drop their claim.'

'Gareth, the media won't be interested if we win anyway,' I say. 'They'll focus on the charges, what the women say you did to them, how you did it and so forth. You've seen what it's been like so far.'

Gareth sits back a long way in the chair and looks out the window again, breathes in and out. 'Okay, let's do it.' Jef Blackwell smiles.

As he's leaving, Gareth grabs my hand as if to shake, then pulls me towards him and embraces me quickly. After he leaves, I see John through the partially open vertical blinds, his eyes even wider than usual, his lips parted.

Later in the day, Daniel strides into my office with Mark Campinelli. 'This is a stiff payment.'

'We knew it would cost,' I say, walking over and closing the door behind them. 'I think we should proceed. So does Jef Blackwell. The publicity's been bad already and it will get worse.'

Mark is sitting at the coffee table. 'Pressing ahead's a

lose-lose situation as far as you're concerned Dan. I agree with Adele.'

Daniel walks to the window. 'You really think this bastard's worth fifty thousand dollars?'

'It's not him, it's our reputation,' I say.

'Great, every time someone makes allegations about us we're going to roll over. This is tough medicine for me Adele.' I watch him walk along next to the window, running his hand over the glass. He walks back and forth three times before he turns to face us. I don't point out to him that he's the one who wanted a settlement, I know he's coming around.

'Looks like I'm outnumbered by advisers.' He sighs and walks over to the coffee table where Mark and I are sitting. He starts to sit then gets up again quickly, stands over us. 'But if it weren't for the quality visit, I'd let him rot. I tell you, I'm going to make that little bastard a bit more careful in future. After this is settled I'm going to see him one on one and tell him what he can and can't do in my university.'

'But you said you thought he was innocent.'

Mark and Daniel look at me. 'What?' Daniel says.

'You told me you thought Jane Kidman was lying, that Gareth would never do anything like this.'

'Of course she was,' Daniel says. 'I'm just pissed about the money.'

# THIRTY-FOUR

The semester ends, it's the middle of winter, ice on the roads, hot chocolate. By the time classes resume, Walters has regained a sense of balance. The media have disappeared. I go through my in-tray, write letters, make calls, go to meetings, tire of administration.

Mummy fades in and out like bad radio reception. Daddy's still around the edges, ephemeral. Others too, Uncle Jack, Auntie Clare. I read an article about cancer of the brain and convince myself I have a tumour. I learn that Alzheimer's disease might be connected to aluminium saucepans. I try to remember our saucepans but I can't.

When I was very little, Uncle Jack bought me some baby chickens, I called them my darlings. I held them in my little arms, kissed them, hugged them, they followed me around the yard. On bad days, I marched them through the house, yelled at them, tortured them into line.

I dream Bill Pozzi is dying of an unknown illness. He tells me he loves me, he's always loved me, I tell him I love him too. I feel good, as if I've finally found the truth. I wake up, feeling really happy, until I realise what I dreamed.

I think of calling Jane Kidman but I don't know what I'd say. I asked Kit Jackson once whether Jane took up our offer of counselling through the equity section. Kit laughed.

I take the senior staff of my division away on a retreat to prepare for the quality visit. We go to an inexpensive beach resort at Rosebud. The food and lodgings are terrible. The

facilitator wears beige pants and large shoes and draws concentric circles on a whiteboard. Gareth and I walk along the
beach one evening, joined by the high-pitched yells of sea-
gulls, the slow roll of sea on shore.

'I have this dream about the sea,' I say. 'It's at night and
there's always a moon. I run into the water to look for
something. I'm not scared exactly, I can see the moon behind
me, yellow through the green water. Then it gets murky and
I can't see the moon. But I'm near what I'm looking for so I
keep swimming. I'm wearing emerald green togs, my body
feels white and exposed. I swim down further and I feel
smaller and smaller. I become scared I'll disappear. I can't
remember what I'm looking for. I start running out of breath.
I wake up scared.'

Gareth says I'm working through something. 'Think of
everything in your dream as some aspect of your self.' There
are rocks at one end of the beach. He suggests we go explor-
ing. We find things, ruby anemones, periwinkles, limpets. He
tells me I'm like a limpet, he pushes one to demonstrate. I
ask him what he means. 'Well defended. I'd like to get in
underneath and find out what's there.'

'A mollusc,' I say. 'Dun-coloured gunk.'

He laughs. 'Exactly my point.' We roll up the legs of our
pants and walk next to the cold black sea. There's enough of
a moon to make small lights in the water, I can see Gareth's
face, the brightness of his eyes, an outline of his dark beard.
He grabs my hand to avoid a wave. We walk the rest of the
way back to the resort in silence, hand in hand. I listen to the
sea.

# THIRTY-FIVE

Daniel is talking about a new remuneration scheme for senior managers. 'We offer an option of a five-year contract appointment in lieu of tenure,' he says. 'At the end of five years, there's no expectation of renewal, it's at our discretion. I know it won't be easy, but there's a carrot. We offer a salary loading to existing managers who'll take a contract. The trick is to make sure the loading is high enough to be attractive to people.'

Daniel, Bill and I are having our regular management meeting, Daniel's idea, these meetings, keeping in touch, touching base. 'I can see where you're heading Dan,' Bill says. 'But it's cultural. Most of our managers expect to be here forever. And we do have some responsibility for them.'

'We can't go on with that assumption Bill. People change. Our needs change. I think it's the only way. What do you think Adele?'

'Where do I sign?' I say.

# THIRTY-SIX

'I can't this weekend Em. I'm going home.'

'Friday night?' she says.

'I've got something on.'

'I never see you anymore.'

Gareth arrives early and we have instant coffee in the foyer. 'I'm really glad you're finally seeing it,' he says.

Inside the theatre there's aqua carpet in large swirling patterns, aqua vinyl seats, a ceiling reminiscent of moonscape photographs, pocked with holes for lights with aqua shades. It's a design feature, the ceiling. The walls are aqua and so is the curtain in front of the screen. It's called the Blue Room.

The film. London, pale summer light, speckles of yellow on green. He dies, she just wants him back, he comes back, as a ghost, she's happy, withdraws from the world, hides at home just to be with him. His ghost friends arrive, watch videos all night every night, she gets sick of them, meets someone else, slowly lets him go, he lets her go. I don't cry.

I love the movies, I feel safe in the dark where anything can happen on a flat bright screen. I love the way the lights come up and go down slowly, the way I can half-close my eyes and make the images flicker at the edge, the giant versions of people. I hate leaving the cinema and I'm still inside with the pale light of London when I see Daniel, walking up the aqua steps with his wife. Gareth sees them, too, and lets go of my hand. 'Adele,' Daniel calls out. Then, with no surprise whatsoever, 'Gareth.'

Daniel's relaxed, he's wearing a soft pink sweatshirt, he has one hand in the pocket of wool trousers. His wife Vicki asks what we've seen, I ask what they're seeing. Gareth tells them *Truly Madly Deeply* is a wonderful film about the grieving process. We make a joke about the decor, I tell them not to drink the coffee. There's a hard lump in the middle of me. They say they better go, they don't want to miss the start.

'That blows my cover,' I say to Gareth with an American accent. 'They'll never believe you're innocent now.'

Gareth laughs. 'Maybe I'm not.' He takes off his glasses, pulls a handkerchief out of his pocket and wipes his face. We go to a coffee shop he knows near the cinema and find a tiny round table with two red chairs in a corner. 'What did you think?' he says.

'I've got mice so I know how she feels.' Rats precipitate the film's central crisis. I ask whether Gareth thinks she only imagines her partner comes back or he really is a ghost.

'Doesn't matter much. To me, it's about coming to terms with hard things, grieving. She brings him back for as long as she needs him, works through her loss, moves on.'

'Do you think people really do that, bring people back to deal with them?'

He says he thought the film would raise feelings about my father for me. 'How are you managing?' I tell him I'm managing okay and I still don't need therapy. He smiles, says it's not therapy, it's the way he is.

'A few months ago, I told Bill Pozzi that Daddy was sick,' I say. 'Only he wasn't, I made it up. I just said it for something to say. And now . . .'

'You're not saying you think in some way you're responsible, are you?'

'No, not that.' I tell him I don't want to talk. He says he respects that. I think again of seeing Daniel, wish I'd been able to avoid it, they'll question my objectivity if the issue ever gets raised again.

Gareth drops me home, walks me to my door, I ask him in for coffee, he says no, he has to pick up Hilary, he kisses me lightly on the lips, holds my arms for a moment and then leaves. I wish he'd stayed for coffee.

# THIRTY-SEVEN

I'm cooking eggs for breakfast on a fine morning, the first for days, and I'm thinking we could go for a walk later. I serve the eggs fried on toast. Mummy clears her throat. 'Adele, there's something I need to tell you. I don't know what might happen to me and there's something you should know about Alain and me.' She never calls Daddy Alain so I get interested. She starts pushing egg around her plate with a fork, making yellow lines. She puts her fork down. 'I'd always meant to tell you. We've always loved you. I couldn't bear the thought of . . .' She trails off, stares wide out the window to Daddy's garden. I hear a strange bird and look over at her but she doesn't seem to have noticed. I sit down on the kitchen side of the bench facing her. 'Do you remember the time Carmel visited all day? You were playing down in the backyard.' Carmel Plunkett was my best friend in primary school. 'You would have been about seven or eight. After she left, you asked me a question. Do you remember?'

'Carmel came over all the time.'

'Carmel said something to you, something about your looking different from Daddy and me. You asked me whether I was really your mother. Remember?'

'I think so,' I lie.

'I said don't be silly, you're my little girl, how else could you be here? You laughed at that. But you were right in a way.' Her voice isn't steady.

'What do you mean?' Her head's on a tilt and I don't like

137

her tone. I want her to stop but I can't manage to tell her that. I want Melbourne and my bed.

'I so much wanted children.' She makes her lips into a line. 'But I didn't get pregnant.' She stops and looks away from me. I don't say anything, I know this story, the miracle of difficult conception. 'It went on and the doctor said be patient, and we were. It was very hard, especially for your father, he saw it so much as his problem. Then someone suggested adoption, so we applied through an agency and waited. Then they told us about a little girl. And there you are. That was you.'

She smiles brightly as if she's just told me something wonderful. I become interested in the physical world. I feel calm, disconnected, the only calm point. I feel a cool breeze through the kitchen window promising spring. Everything's bright, very bright, like Christmas morning, information coming from a long way off. I look down at my eggs which don't seem possible in the circumstances, bizarre like two slimy breasts with giant nipples staring out at me. 'How is that possible?' I sound tinny.

'They said sometimes when there are problems a baby fixes them and then you can conceive. But it didn't happen and I didn't care. You were enough for me. You were all I ever wanted.'

'Why didn't you tell me?' I am reasonable, even, slow.

'I was waiting for the right time. Your father felt there was no point. He said you were our daughter legally, he felt strongly we shouldn't tell you. Even so, I always meant to. But time got away, you grew up, and I couldn't see any point. Now it's different. If I died and you didn't know, or if you found out from someone else. I'm so sorry Adele if I did the wrong thing, but I was never sure what to do. I thought you might hate me.'

'Do Uncle Jack and Auntie Clare know?' She nods yes. 'And Grandma and Grandpa?'

'We told them not to say anything to you. We said we'd tell you in our own time.'

I've read books about families and secrets, I've imagined

things about my family. Not this. It's not that I'm shocked, I'm not even surprised, not really. It's like I've come down through the years with most of a picture that my mother's sweet voice finishes for me. Her telling comes to me from years ago like a confirmation, a handshake. I manage to eat my eggs which taste like eggs. I wash up. My mother is in a state, needing comfort but I just feel tired. All I can think of is getting out with as little fuss as I can manage. 'No Mummy, really, I'm fine. I just want to get home. I've a lot to do.'

'Adele, I love you. I only did what I thought was best.'

She wants me to forgive her. I can't stand her need for forgiveness. 'It's okay Mummy, really, I just need to do some things.'

I drive home with the window down and let cold air slap my face. At home, I get into bed, empty my mind, slow, slow, slow. I feel like layers of opaque material. I sleep. I dream of rats getting into the flat and biting me, only they don't really hurt. It's cold and late in the day when I wake up. The windows are open and I lie in bed for a long while. For the first time since his death, I really miss Daddy, his bumpy feet, his raspiness. I want him to tell me it's just Mummy being silly.

I used to suspend a blanket between the backs of two lounge chairs to build a cubby house. I'd get in there with my toys, host dinners, chat, hide. It was my safe place then. My flat is warm and dark and it reminds me of that place. I feel giddy when I stand up and I lean against the wall for a moment before I go out to the kitchen. I turn on the light, blind myself. I fill the kettle and sit down with it. I must sit there for a while because I become aware of late afternoon noises—cars on the beach road, people walking along the footpath—changing to night noises, neighbours moving around their houses, voices. I'm aware I'm still holding onto the handle of the kettle. I make coffee. I eat chocolate and cold fried rice from the fridge.

I call Gareth. I don't know what else to do. He says it's incredible and tells me to meet him at his place. I don't know what time it is. I don't know how I find the house. He meets me outside, takes me to a room downstairs. I notice that his hair is uncombed and he's wearing a cardigan but underneath he has a vest over a flannel shirt that's not tucked in properly. His breath smells metallic like sleep. There are no lights on in the upstairs part of the house.

'Is this your office?'

'It's easier with Hilary to work from home.'

He's sitting facing me, forward, elbows on his knees, hands clasped in front. He says I need time to integrate what's happened. I'm shaking, cold, sobbing, I say I don't feel like me. Gareth grabs my hand, sits me down on the floor between his knees. 'Let it out,' he says. He rocks me gently while I cry. 'It's all right, I'm here, it's all right.' I don't know how long I sit there. His arms enclose me and the smell of his body is strangely reassuring. When I get up, he embraces me lightly, kisses me on the forehead, leaves his kiss there for a moment, then holds me at arm's length. 'That was great.'

'I feel as if I should be managing better. I know I need to call Mummy, tell her I'm all right, but I can't bring myself to talk to her at the moment.'

'Take your time, she'll still be there.'

When I leave Gareth it's late and I feel sad but less fallen apart.

At 7 am, Emily turns up uninvited with croissants. She's on her way home from work in a good mood because they cancelled her transfer, so she can stay in the cancer ward. 'What you need is a holiday,' she says. I watch as she measures scoops of coffee and tips them into the plunger. I don't offer to help.

I have this repeating sensation like a loud noise hitting me in the chest. My parents have hidden this from me, hidden this from me. Hidden this from me to soothe themselves. Is this anger? Emily is talking and I've missed some. 'When I rang, the guy said we couldn't get a booking until late in February.'

There would have been a full birth certificate somewhere. Did I never see it? There would have been letters from the government, especially when the legislation changed. I was a teenager then. But I never received them. Did they hide them? Did I ask questions? Did they lie? Did they all lie? My parents, Uncle Jack, all of them? I did ask questions, about the hospital, about childbirth, about where I came from. All those stories about my premature arrival, my mother in the hospital. And my birth certificate, I remember asking Mummy for one, she gave me an extract, told me that was all there was. I believed her. I believed her. All those comments people made about how different we looked. All those lies. All those lies. I reinvent my life. Everything.

'Adele?' Emily is sitting opposite and looking at me.

'Sorry. What were you saying?'

'What do you think?'

'About what?'

'The trip, Tasmania.'

'Fine. When?'

'I just told you, February.'

'Sorry Em, I was daydreaming.'

'Well, what about it?'

'Fine, fine, you just get it.'

'Adele, are you okay?'

'Yeah.' She doesn't believe me but she doesn't pry either.

After Emily leaves I call work, tell John I'm not well, I won't be in. I go back to my bedroom, sit on the end of my bed, stare into the mirror, move right up close, my lips almost touching. My eyes are dark brown but I have trouble relating this to things I know. My skin looks sallow in the morning light. My hair is dark and all over my face. I stare and stare, wanting to understand. I'm not who I thought. Is that it? I see my nose and find it hard to place. It's on my face but not my face. I move back, watch my torso, rustling flannel pyjamas. I'm so much bigger than them, towering over them with my obviousness, bigger than my life. I move closer again. I'm not like you I whisper to the mirror, forming fog around the new reflection of my mouth.

# THIRTY-EIGHT

Mummy calls me twice a day for a week, at work and at home, she talks about nothing, the weather, the garden, the extension to Jack's house, then she gets teary, asks when I'll be visiting, tells me she loves me, she's always loved me. I feel strangled by her love, I tell her I'm all right, I just need some time, I feel unsure about things, I need to think.

Uncle Jack visits the flat, tells me he's sorry. 'I just wish someone had told me,' I say.

'I wanted to tell you, but it wasn't my place.'

'Who's place was it?'

'I'd be angry too.'

Gareth calls. 'How are you really?'

'You know the most incredible thing? When she told me, I wasn't all that surprised. It's as if I knew something wasn't quite right. It's like, so that's it, that's the mystery. I just wish they'd said.'

He says he understands. 'I found a couple of books you might be interested in.' I say thanks. 'You really need to talk this through Adele.' I agree.

I go to his house in St Kilda. There's a sign on the door that says *Gareth Ford—Counsellor*. I go through to a small entrance hall that serves as a waiting area. A boy is sitting there with long greasy hair and a pierced ear. He couldn't be more than eleven or twelve. I stare at the closed door. He stares at me. We hear muffled voices within. Gareth is twenty minutes late. He emerges behind a woman. They hug for several moments then the woman and boy leave.

He smiles. 'I'm glad you decided to come.' We go into the office, sit down, I take a chair with wooden arms, he sits opposite me, in a leather recliner. I say me too, feel awkward. He stops smiling, lights a cigarette, asks what's happening. I tell him I feel all right, he nods slowly. There's a pause, then I say I think I'm coming to terms with it, I just wish they'd told me earlier. I say I've always felt different from them anyway. I tell him I wish I'd known before Daddy died. I don't want to hurt them but I don't know what to say to them.

He says an important piece of information has been missing for me, information I needed in order to live my life. He says he understands. He tells me it's okay to be angry, it's okay not to think of my family for a while, he tells me to think about what I want for myself, he sounds just like Emily. He says he's interested that I've always felt different from my family. He asks me how different, leans forward to hear my answer. I tell him I feel too big, too big and stupid, like I'm the wrong one. I sort of spit the words out, surprise myself with how angry I feel. Then I can't talk, I just cry and cry. He moves us down to the floor, wraps his arms around me. I don't know how long we sit there. Eventually he tells me it's time to finish, he asks me how I feel. 'I feel safe,' I say.

He smiles. 'You're going to work really fast. It's all there Adele.' I ask him about money. 'What do you mean?'

'For the counselling,' I say.

'That's friendship, I couldn't possibly accept payment.'

# THIRTY-NINE

Therapy. Months. A warm room, faded carpet, old chairs, the smell of tobacco. His kind face, smiling, caring, watching. Me in pieces.

Sometimes I imagine someone in the lounge chair opposite me—Mummy, Daddy, Uncle Jack—and talk to them. Sometimes I play the part of me. Then I switch chairs and play the part of whoever I've been imagining in the lounge chair. I carry on conversations with these people who've been in my head for so long. He tells me this is empty chair work. I say it's funny, I've spent most of the last year doing empty chair work, worrying I might be crazy because my parents appear in my head. Now he tells me it's therapeutic. He smiles. 'Think of that earlier stuff as preparation for this,' he gestures towards the empty chair. 'Let's get back to work.'

Sometimes I sit on the floor between Gareth's legs, he holds me, soothes, says there there while I cry and cry and cry. I never knew I had all these tears. I write things down, thoughts, dreams, fears, I fill an exercise book. I buy books from the self-help section, healing the child within, bad things happening to good people, my treacherous heart, my toxic parents.

It starts to feel like a footnote, adoption, a tiny footnote that explains an important paragraph. It's the paragraph that matters, but the paragraph doesn't make much sense without the footnote. Gareth says I'm working quickly because I was so ready. He says I'd done all the preliminaries with my parents in my head. He says I won't be able to grieve my father's death until I know who he was to me. He says I shouldn't have contact with my mother at this time. He says Jack let me down. He says I'll be finished soon.

I start to understand that it has meant everything, adoption, everything and nothing. For the first time, I tell myself I'm all right and mean it. I start to feel I might know what I want. And through it all, Gareth is a constant. I feel closer to him than anyone alive and yet, I hardly know him.

I call Mummy, tell her I want space and time. I talk to Uncle Jack, tell him I feel betrayed by him. He says he'd like to see me. I tell him no, not yet.

I reinvent my real mother dark and mysterious or just like me. I imagine her over and over again. I say to Gareth, 'I've decided I want to meet my birth mother.' He says he can understand that, helps me find the adoption agency, tells me I'm on my journey.

# FORTY

John walks into my office, closes the door and hands me the text of an email message.

> I talked to a few people about your counsellor. Seems there was a problem some years ago, one very poor student (later gross failed) said he favoured female students. He was otherwise okay, well connected, very popular, good teacher. We'd employ him again so I can't see any reason for you to worry. Good luck.

It's from Desmond Cooper, the VC at Bass University, to Daniel, dated some months ago, when we were in the middle of the investigation. 'Where did you get this?'

'VC's email trash.'

'You don't have access.'

'I'm training the temp in his office. She has his email password. Yesterday I was pulling stuff out of the trash to show her how to recover it when I saw this. The subject was Gareth Ford so when she went to answer a phone call, I printed it back here. I thought it might be important.'

'Thanks John but I've already seen this.' I read the message again. At best it's equivocal, it doesn't really say anything and Daniel said Gareth checked out okay at Bass. But he could have told me there were questions, he could have mentioned it, given me a chance to follow up. 'Anything else?' I notice John is still standing there. He looks at me, says no and walks out quickly.

# FORTY-ONE

I arrive for my appointment with Joan Lynch five minutes early. The address she gave me over the phone is a run down brick building near the women's hospital, an ex-government building among government buildings. I walk up two flights of stairs to a reception area and press a buzzer that's louder than it looks. Some minutes later a squat woman with short wavy grey hair comes out of an office. 'You must be Adele,' she says.

Joan's office is small, two plastic chairs facing the door and a small desk with a third chair behind it. There are fluorescent lights above us. She sits behind the desk and tells me she's there to help. She looks like a rotund nurse, light blue belted dress, watch pinned to her chest, only the red scarf out of place. Forced fast smile, as if she puts it over something else.

'I know how difficult this must be for you,' she says. 'But you mustn't blame your adoptive parents. They did what they thought was best. We thought it was better to keep things just between us and the parents. We thought it confused children. It's different now of course. The legislation for one thing, but also, our thoughts about child development and so forth.'

She takes my hand. I take it back. 'I'm sorry,' I say. 'I really just want to know who my parents are.' I smile. 'I understand I have a right to that information.'

'Of course you do and we need to talk about that.'

Joan has a file on her desk with the letters L A N pasted down one side in red plastic tape. I realise this is my file, I have a file. 'Joan, I don't mean to be rude but I don't really want to talk. I'm seeing a counsellor who's helping me work through my adoption. What I'm wanting from you is any information you have about my parents. As far as I'm concerned we can do that one of two ways. You can tell me now, or I can write to the Department of Community Services.'

Joan stops smiling. 'I can understand your wanting to know quickly,' she says. 'I just want to make sure you're prepared. This is very difficult for people.' She sits up straight. 'As you'd know, you're required to attend an interview before anyone can give you information. I'm just trying to do the right thing in accordance with the Act.'

'I appreciate that.'

She makes her lips into two fat little slugs. She's angry with me and I don't care. She picks up the file on her desk and proceeds to tell me in a monotone about my life. She says she'll provide me with copies of documents, my birth certificate, the adoption order, reports from social workers on my progress, but there will be a small charge. She has a photograph of me as a baby in hospital, the same as the one I saw at home on the kitchen bench. Joan explains that they took it in case my birth mother ever asked for it. She didn't. She parcels all these documents into a blank envelope and hands it to me.

When I leave, it's late afternoon on a day that's turned from rain to soft yellow sunshine. I've forgotten my coat but I hardly notice the cold. Everything is slow. I am slow. I can hear traffic and from time to time, it gets louder and comes right into my body. I am still. I am all over the world.

It's dark by the time I get back to the office. In my bag are the photocopies for which I've paid a small charge. I didn't take the photograph. In case my mother ever wanted it. I pick up my in-tray and start towards the door just as Bill Pozzi appears.

'Adele, I've been looking for you, the schedule's good, everyone's ready, well done.'

'What?'

'The quality visit next week, the rehearsal today. Did you forget?'

'Yeah, I had something else on. Did it go well?'

'We pulled in everyone who's meeting the visiting commit- tee. Daniel told them it's like an oral, we've submitted the thesis and now they're coming for a viva.' Bill smiles. 'He told them this is our watershed, our year, the year for stu- dents.' He shakes his head slowly. He doesn't leave and I don't know what to say. 'I think things are back on track Adele,' he says finally. He walks over and goes to pat me on the arm but misses and somehow gets my head. 'Sorry.'

'That's okay. Back on track Bill.'

'Sure are,' he winks and starts to leave slowly.

I call him back. 'Did you know I was adopted?'

He's standing at my door and he turns around and looks at me. 'Yes, your father and I were with the firm at the time.'

'They should have told me.'

'They didn't?' I shake my head no. He walks back into the office, looks at me for a moment. 'I imagine it would have been hard for them.' He smiles. 'Your dad was so happy when you arrived. Like a big kid. I don't think he thought about where you came from. He was just so proud of you.'

'He lied to me.'

'Of course he did, like all parents lie to their children and all children lie to their parents. You're saying he breached trust, he had a duty to tell you. But think of it from his point of view. It wasn't part of his framework. All he saw was his wonderful daughter who he loved so much.'

I drive home and the photocopies remain in my satchel like something alive, growing bigger and heavier in spite of me.

# FORTY-TWO

'She's a school teacher,' I say. 'They describe her as intelligent and determined. I get the impression that she's been through a lot. There's stuff in the file about her family. Her father's a writer, her mother's French, like Daddy, she's got a brother, they live in Queensland. There's nothing about the birth father.'

When we finish Gareth hugs me gently. 'Let's go to dinner tonight to celebrate.'

'To celebrate what?'

'You.'

We walk to a Chinese restaurant round the corner from my flat. Gareth's more himself tonight, less concerned with my problems. He talks about Hilary. 'She's obsessed with ducks. Wakes up in the morning thinking about them. I'm going to take her to the gardens with some bread. Want to come?' He grabs my hand. 'I've had a lovely night. I hope we'll be friends for a long time.'

'Me too.'

After dinner we walk along the pier. It's blustery and he wraps me in his coat.

'You've helped me so much,' I say.

'You're the one who did the work, I just nodded at the right times.'

'I never thought I'd like therapy.'

'I've been more like a skilled friend than a therapist. You'd have managed all this without me.'

'I don't think so.'

'You've helped me too you know. It's not a one-way thing.'

We go back to my flat, I walk through to the sitting room and offer coffee, tell him to sit down. He doesn't, he follows me into the kitchen. I light the gas and put the kettle on. 'I thought once of committing suicide with gas,' I say. I smile, this seems so far away from where I am now that I can hardly believe it was the same me.

'Really,' he says. He's standing in the doorway to the kitchen and the fluorescent light makes us look like ghosts. I go to the refrigerator to get milk. He walks over to where I am, grabs the cyclic defrost door, trapping me with his thin arms between the open refrigerator and the bench. 'Adele, I need to talk with you.' He looks serious.

'Last time someone said that to me I found out my parents weren't really my parents.' I try to laugh but he's still looking at me, he's not laughing. 'What?'

'I'm really attracted to you Adele. I know this sounds crazy after everything that's happened but I've liked you since the first day I walked into your office. I feel I have to tell you.' He's looking at my face, my mouth I think. There's a vein just under his left eye that I've never noticed before. Perhaps it's become prominent with this mood.

How do I feel? I feel as if I'd like to fall into his arms and let him hold me. I need so much of what he's offering that I wonder if he'll be able to cope. He leans over towards me and starts to kiss me. He's so soft.

I become aware of a high pitched sound that at first I think is in my head. Gareth is kissing me all over my neck and chest. He continues to frame me in a diamond made of his arms and the open refrigerator. 'The kettle,' I say. He releases me. I go over and switch off the stove. I'm relieved when he closes the refrigerator. Then he takes my hand and leads me across the hallway into the sitting room. We sit on the couch.

'I like you Adele and I think you like me too.' I don't say anything exactly, I sort of grunt. He pulls me towards him and kisses my mouth. I feel uncoordinated.

I sit back. 'Gareth this is all a bit fast, I didn't realise.'

'I'll show you something.' He stands up, takes off his belt. 'Grab the other end of this.' I do, he pulls it, so do I. 'See, we all need something.' This reminds me of something else but I can't remember what. He puts his belt back on, sits down beside me, joins his hands in a sort of prayer above his knees. 'I guess I've been thinking about this for weeks. I forgot I've only just told you about it. Tell me how you're feeling.' I can see the outline of strong arms through his sweater.

I think of Jane Kidman, the look on her face when she came to see me the second time, that momentary kiddish grin quickly replaced by something older and sadder. I say, 'I'm just thinking about Jane.'

'I think about her all the time.'

'Nothing happened, did it?'

He shakes his head slowly, opens his mouth and closes it again then speaks. 'Adele, we've talked about this. Someone getting too close is really scary for you isn't it?' He's right. I am scared. He's looking at my eyes. 'I want to make love with you, but I don't want to do anything you don't want to do.' He shifts hair out of my face, moves to hold me, strokes my back gently, says it's all right.

It's dark in the sitting room and I haven't turned on the gas heater. I lift my face to his and kiss him, his lips, neck, closed eyes, ears. After some time, I get up and take him to my room. We undress quickly, kiss again, climb into bed. He's gentle, holds me, strokes my back, my breasts, shoulders, belly. He smells dry and his fingers are long and soft. I am my skin. I keep feeling centred in different parts of my body. Small bits become large and extensive bits become minute.

I wake up. Gareth says he has to go. 'Adele, this is great. I just love you.' He kisses me on the forehead, holds my head in his two hands for a moment, jumps off the bed, punches the air, comes back down on the bed, kisses me again. 'I love you.' Then he says he'll see me tomorrow.

I go back to my room. I look in my mirror at myself. I'm smiling, serious, me from the front, the side. I take off my shirt and look at my breasts, my hips, dark pubic hair and legs. I must sit there staring in the mirror for a long time, the morning starts. I feel as if I really know something but I don't know what it is.

# FORTY-THREE

Emily drops over on her way home from work. We drink hot chocolate in the kitchen and I tell her about the mouse I can't kill. 'I'm going to buy a gun and sit up and wait.'

'You'll fall asleep and shoot yourself.' She looks around the kitchen. 'Haven't seen you for a bit.' I tell her I'm seeing a therapist. 'That's fantastic Adele,' she says. 'But how the mighty fall.' I used to criticise Emily's therapy. 'What's his name?'

'Gareth.'

'Not the guy who had sex with that student.'

'He was found not guilty, he didn't do it.'

'I could have given you some names.'

'He's more of a friend than a therapist. '

'A friend.' She looks at me. 'You're not screwing him are you?'

'I said I like him.'

I get the feeling Emily wants to say more but decides against it. Just before she leaves she says, 'If you want the name of a proper therapist, give me a call.'

I'm sweating under blankets when the phone rings, it must be around four. It's the night security manager from the university. 'There's been an accident,' he says. 'A fall from the tower.' He's following procedures—call the registrar, call the police, call PR.

Approaching from any direction, the Walters University Business Tower demands your attention. It's out of place here,

154

0

154

surrounded by older buildings, sharing a courtyard of elms and grass with redbrick history. A skinny straight glass and granite rod. The architects said they wanted a fundamental contrast. You'd have to accept they achieved it.

Someone got into the Tower on Sunday night, a security lapse in itself given its communication and security system, someone got in there and fell, from the top to the cement courtyard below, fell and crumpled and died. 'I'll be there as soon as I can.'

There's ice on the windscreen and my breath smokes. I call Daniel from the car. 'We've got a problem,' I say. He keeps saying My God.

When I arrive the police and ambulance are already there. People moving around in the red and blue lights give the courtyard a slow motion disco atmosphere. The police are investigating—holding polystyrene cups in two hands, stepping to keep warm, setting up floodlights, building a barrier around the scene. The ambulance people are waiting quietly. It's a long time before the sun comes up. I ask them to remove the body before people start arriving for classes.

She looks amazingly unhurt, she must have turned during the fall, like a reverse cat, or maybe she fell backwards, because she's face up, eyes staring, splayed on the cement. There's some blood but I don't know where from. Her hair is still red which for some reason surprises me. I don't watch her for too long.

Mark Campinelli's beside me. 'We've got to have a statement ready.'

The man who's in charge asks me to go with his officers to tell the parents. He has a blue speckled wool jumper and corduroy trousers and his black hair is sticking up at the back. He says it's better if there's someone there from her life. I ride in a police car. No siren, two police in front not saying much. I discover you can't open the back door from the inside.

The parents are much smaller than I thought they'd be. He's old and bent, looking at us is an effort, two or three sad pieces of hair fall onto his forehead. She's thin and grey in the skin. They're in proper pyjamas and dressing gowns with slippers. There are faded roses on the carpet. She's their only child. They're dignified about it. They don't blame anyone yet. He agrees to go to identify the body. She says she wants to go too. A doctor appears while we're there, offering sedatives.

By the time I get home to shower and change, it's 7 am and the sun has come up into a pink and yellow sky. The radio news doesn't mention her by name, doesn't mention the court case or the settlement, doesn't mention the university much at all. So no one says we killed her. But it's a beautiful day and Jane Kidman is dead all the same.

At work, Daniel is managing a situation. The quality review committee is coming today, he's walking too quickly around my office, talking softly as if he's calm. I'm sitting at my desk, Bill stands near me, his hand on my shoulder. Daniel says he wants to keep things quiet. 'Adele we have to pull together.'

The office seems ethereal, light, without context. 'I saw her,' I say.

He says he knows. 'It's awful, just awful, but we've got to do our best. This is the day it all comes together for you, it's your day.'

Bill tells him to leave me alone. 'Dan, don't you know what this means?'

I say I'm okay, I just need time, I ask them to leave me for a while, I sit at my desk, speed up and slip into some other self. John comes in with coffee, asks if I'm all right, I tell him later, not now. I go to Walters House and greet the visiting committee, five experts who look like the future. Daniel, Bill and I stumble through the first session, Daniel takes the lead, the more I force myself to be present, the less real the night's events become. Then it's easy. The program runs like clockwork, ten sessions with eight staff and students in each. Gareth Ford leads the group of counselling staff, that was my idea, weeks ago, he impresses the visitors with his commitment to students and the high quality of our counselling services. At the end of the day, the experts tell Daniel we're the university that offers the student a complete package—

course and career guidance, personal counselling, study skills, graduate support—*The university that values students.* They commend us for our submission and especially for the work of our Counselling department.

# FORTY-FOUR

The funeral, bright yellow sunshine in a cobalt sky, everything in pictures. Daniel Reed and Bill Pozzi, standing together in dark suits like a charcoal drawing, other staff, twenty or so, like a watercolour. Students, hundreds of students, like an abstract, colour and sound and brightness. The priest in white with gold like a gothic, the smell of incense, the full-size white coffin, the eulogy, delivered by Jane's best friend, bejewelled and gypsy-like. The press, how can they do this, their cameras, microphones, TV station T-shirts and leather jackets, their obviousness, their garish obviousness.

It's nothing like Daddy's funeral, less formal and more obviously sad. I think of him though, I think of what he'd say to me now.

Daniel wrote a beautiful letter to the Kidmans, about his own children, about loss, about how nothing could ever heal, about God and the power of love. Bill visited them, more than once.

We're chased by the media who want to know why we're not taking action against Gareth Ford. 'That's over,' Daniel tells them, 'and unrelated.' He says it's the most unfortunate incident of his academic career. He says he is deeply saddened to lose a student in such circumstances, his heart goes out to the Kidmans in their loss. He says he doesn't know what they're talking about when they talk about Gareth Ford. He says that Gareth has nothing to do with this tragic, tragic story.

Gareth comes to my office. He tells me the press have been

at him. 'This is a nightmare. I thought of contacting Jane a few weeks ago, I thought things weren't great for her, the person she was seeing wasn't much good. I thought she could come and see me. But the lawyers said it would compromise the settlement. I could have prevented this, I know I could. And now . . .' He trails off in tears. 'Poor little Jane.' He sits there, crying openly now. I hand him a tissue. I don't say anything.

Emily asks the question. 'If he didn't do it, why did she kill herself?'

# FORTY-FIVE

I leave home early, there's an accident at St Kilda, red and blue lights, a young police officer directing traffic, she's wearing a yellow vest with a white X on the front, looks nervous, as if she's not sure the cars will do what they're told and the X is a target. I give her a little wave. She ignores me.

It's quiet on the fifth floor at this time, the cleaners have already gone home, I switch on some lights on the way through. I go to my desk and find the print of the email John gave me from Desmond Cooper to Daniel. Daniel said there were no problems at Bass, that Cooper gave Gareth the all clear. But it wasn't all clear, there was a problem, there were questions. I was the investigator, Daniel should have told me, given me a chance.

I knew there was something about Gareth's appointment, something I missed, something to do with referees, something to do with Bass. I call Helen Yates in Central Records. 'You remember those searches we did a few months ago on Gareth Ford's former employers and referees?' She does. 'Still got the list?' She has. 'Anyone from Bass Uni?' She says yes, she told me that before.

'I'll get the list.' She drops the phone noisily. I say hi to John who's just arrived. He startles, then says hello. This is a long shot, the referee reports were destroyed, Jim Berry told me that. Helen comes back to the phone. 'There are 50 letters from Bass University.' I tell her I'm coming down, I want to see the files.

I walk around the elevator, feeling charged, singing some-thing I heard on the radio this morning. Helen has already pulled a pile of thick files out of the compactus. 'They're still marked,' she says. 'You didn't look at them last time.' She clicks her tongue.

Most of the letters are on planning or management files, nothing to do with Gareth Ford. There's a single letter from a Janet Myerson that looks promising on the listing Helen provides because it's on a staff conditions file. When I find the letter, it turns out that Janet was a visiting academic from Bass who was paid at the wrong rate. A dead end. The other name I check is Rupert Haynes, a psychologist who's a member of one of our committees. There are seventeen letters from him, mostly on course and policy files. Helen brings over the rest of the files, mostly to do with the Psychology course. Nothing nothing nothing.

Then I find it. It's on a staff recruitment policy file. It's a letter from Rupert Haynes, addressed to the vice-chancellor.

Sir

I am writing to point out to you a concern I have about selection processes at your university. Several months ago, a colleague used my name as a referee for a position at Walters. I provided a favourable report as this partic-ular colleague was one of the best in my department. In good conscience though, I raised a concern I regarded as important in relation to the position. In particular, I suggested that perhaps my colleague wasn't ready for a move to the particular area of the profession where he was seeking work.

I was surprised to find that not only were my com-ments ignored (no one contacted me to follow up). My colleague has been appointed to the position and is now in post.

I am not writing this letter to ask that any action be taken in terms of the particular instance, I only want to point out to you the general concern I have about your

selection processes. At my university, we take our referees seriously.

Yours sincerely,

Professor Rupert Haynes

It's addressed to Daniel who's referred it to the registrar with
a note, 'Registrar, please handle.' Tom McIntyre would have
been back by then.

Tom's written, 'NFA'. NFA. NFA means no further action.
Of course, Tom wasn't on the selection panel, I was, and if
you weren't on the selection panel, you wouldn't know where
to start. Haynes could be referring to any one of a hundred
panels. I guess Tom could have done a search for Haynes'
name. But I suppose he reckoned we'd made an appointment,
it was too late. Why bother trying to find a good reference
coded with a secret message? But NFA, NFA, no further
action. No further action? Why didn't he mention it, couldn't
he have asked?

I remember the referee report now, it had some vague
statement about whether Gareth was ready for the move to
counselling young students. I think someone on the panel
even made a joke about the difference between young and
old students. The agreement in the selection panel was that
I'd ring Haynes and check, and if there were any concerns I'd
get the panel back together. But I never rang him, I decided
it wasn't important. You get a million of these things. With
freedom of information laws people are nervous about writing
all good or all bad references. I decided not to do anything
even before we left the meeting room. I didn't do anything
and then we appointed Gareth.

And then Haynes' letter went to Daniel who referred it to
Tom McIntyre. And then Tom wrote no further action. And
then Daniel told me Gareth was fine in Adelaide and I wanted
that to be true. And then I failed to investigate properly.

And here I am.

Whoever answers the phone tells me Professor Rupert
Haynes is the head of the Psychology department. I leave a
message. He gets back almost straight away. He says he's been

wondering when he might hear from us. He's pretentious which makes things worse. He says he was sending a warning. 'Nothing was ever proven. I couldn't say he was sleeping with his students when nothing was proven. But there was talk. There was too much talk.'

I think of saying to him that his reference didn't exactly give a very strong hint but I don't. I question him closely, there were no formal complaints, nothing was formally alleged, he just heard around the department that Gareth Ford was smelly. 'You get to know people like that.'

Jane Kidman's lawyers found Rupert Haynes by accident when they were researching Gareth Ford's history. 'I told them I'd written you and they said they wanted me to appear.'

Bill was right. In the legal case, he was a third party so there was no obligation to provide a copy of his letter as part of the discovery process. The first we'd have seen of him would have been at trial. Neat.

I get off the phone as soon as I can. 'I'm going to shut my door and work quietly for a while John.' He says okay, looks at me as if I've lost my mind. 'What?' He says it's nothing. 'Good, then don't look like it's something.'

He follows me into the office. 'Is there anything I can do to help?'

I'm just about to yell at him to get out when I see his face. He wears these glasses that enlarge his eyes ridiculously, he parts his hair too far to one side. He looks so vulnerable, so kind. I realise I've been wrong about him. I've been wrong about everything. 'I'm sorry John, I really am. I'm just having a really bad time.' My voice cracks on really bad and I almost cry. He takes a tissue from the box on my coffee table.

'That's okay,' he says. 'Let me know if I can help.' He hands me the tissue.

# FORTY-SIX

The truth. I hate the truth. When I get to Gareth's house, I wish I could make the truth go away. 'I have to ask you something,' I say. We're in his office, I can hear Hilary upstairs.

'What is it?' He looks so sweet, uplines on his forehead, his eyes wide, mouth half open. We're sitting at the coffee table, I'm in the least comfortable chair, the empty-chair-work chair.

'There's not a nice way to ask really. There's so much happening. You and me. Jane Kidman, work, my family. I haven't been thinking very well for such a long while.'

'It's Jane, isn't it? You want to know about Jane.'

'Do I?' And then he tells me. He tells me in a deep flat voice like someone else. He had sex with her in his office, just like she told us. She consented. She even initiated. He stumbles over the word seduce as if he's not really used to it. He says he really loved her, he knows that what he did was wrong, he didn't have sex with any other client.

'I breached my ethics with Jane Kidman, I realise that. I know what I did. I know the price.' I ask him why he didn't tell me. He says he wanted to. 'I even tried during the case, but you didn't want to know.' I think about this and it's probably true. 'Then when I realised I was falling in love with you, I couldn't tell you. I thought you'd hate me. It's been eating away at me.' He doesn't look like he's being eaten. I ask about Adelaide. He says what about it. I say there was talk there, too. He says not that he knew of. 'My approach is still considered pretty different. There's always talk about someone like me. Jane Kidman's the only client I've ever fallen in love with. And I did love her. That's why I stopped therapy.'

'How do you expect me to believe you?'

'What you believe is up to you. I'm telling the truth. I've got no reason to lie.' He grabs for my hand, I pull away. 'Adele, I'm not some evil monster. I made a mistake, I went off the rails. That's all.'

'Jane Kidman is dead.'

'I'm not responsible for Jane Kidman's life.' I don't say anything. 'I was Jane's psychotherapist, I contracted to work with her, I stuck to process, she did good work. Then I breached my ethics, I messed up the countertransference. But I didn't kill her. She killed herself.' I don't say anything. 'What if I was incompetent and she killed herself? Would that be my fault, too? I'm willing to take responsibility for what I did. But I didn't kill Jane Kidman. That's Jane's responsibility.'

'You lied at the misconduct committee.'

'Haven't you ever lied when you've been scared about something? You know you have. That story you told about your father being sick. Is it really so different from me? My work's good. I think I've helped you although you might like to reconstruct that now.' He's right about this, he has helped me. 'I know what I did was wrong. I know it was wrong to lie. But I'm telling the truth when I say it's the first time in my life I've done that. And I'll never do it again.'

I don't have anything I can say. I tell him I'm leaving. 'What are you going to do?' he says.

'I don't know Gareth, I just don't know.'

# FORTY-SEVEN

I feel safe when I fly. I like the world of the aeroplane, the rush at take-off, the enclosed seats and bubble windows, the drop-down, mid-flight video entertainment, the little plastic cups and tiny bottles of label wine, the gourmet meals in their compact airline food trays, the basket of hot bread rolls. It's a miniature world. I love to fly. I never feel nervous when I fly.

We agreed to meet at a cafe on the Gold Coast, at the end of a long arcade on a tongue of sand along a large canal called a spit. It was her idea, the Gold Coast, she said it was appropriate. From the deck where I sit, I can see parasailors on the far bank, blobs of colour thrown onto the blue blue sky. Everything is bright, there are no clouds, I can feel sweat all over me like honey. I don't feel nervous, I feel relaxed and she's late.

She walks over to the table quickly and I recognise her straight away. She's older than I thought, about my height, slimmer than me but not slim. She wears jeans and a white T-shirt. Her hair is long and dark brown going grey. Her skin is fair and her eyes are brown. She doesn't smile. For a moment, but only for a moment, I wonder if that idiot social worker in Melbourne made a mistake.

We say hello, stare at each other a bit like lovers do. I have a feeling she's looking for something but I don't know what. She says her name is Marilyn Ferguson. 'I thought you'd be younger,' she says. Her voice is warm and full.

'Me too,' I say. 'I mean I thought you'd be younger.' We laugh but it fades quickly.

She taps on the table lightly with one finger, orders a gin and tonic, lights a cigarette. 'Here we are.' I say yes, here we are. I tell her I appreciate her making time for me, I imagine it would be hard for her. She smiles but I don't get the impression it's an easy smile. I say I found out about my adoption recently, after my father's death. She frowns, it passes quickly. There's a pause. I can hear a motor boat out on the water and music starts up from speakers inside the cafe, loud music that gets louder every time a waiter opens the door. I hear an excited happy male voice over a microphone. A fashion parade.

I say, 'I'd be really interested in knowing about you. Anything you feel you can tell me.'

'Yes,' she drains her glass and motions to our waiter. 'I've been thinking about that.' She takes a deep breath, blows it out and sits up straighter in her chair. This is difficult for her, and prepared, too, in some way, like a set piece that she's worked up. She talks without inflection, reporting facts. She tells me she's a teacher at a Catholic school in Brisbane. English and French. I tell her I'm a university administrator. She looks at me from time to time as if she wants to ask me things but doesn't.

She tells me she was born and grew up in Toowoomba, west of Brisbane. Her family's French Catholic on her mother's side, just like Daddy. She went to Catholic schools, boarded in secondary, just like me. She says her father was a writer who taught at college. His family's from Scotland. He was a lot older than her mother, she says he was witty and fun to be with. I ask what he looked like. She says she has some pictures, she takes a white envelope out of her bag, hands me two photographs.

The first is of her father she says, my grandfather, as a boy. His name is Andrew. He has soft looking hair and eyes, the beginnings of a moustache like dirt over his top lip. He wears long grey trousers and a white cotton shirt that isn't tucked in properly. His feet stick out on an angle. He isn't smiling and gives the impression that he doesn't want the photograph to be taken. He has a wistfulness I find rather appealing.

The second photograph, taken years later, is of Andrew and his wife, her mother, my grandmother. Her name is Michelle. Andrew is holding a baby, my mother's older brother, my uncle Mark. Mark's face is flushed and frowning. He might have been crying. Andrew is older, bald on top of his head and hunched and thin in the shoulders. He's wearing a suit with a vest. His feet still poke out on an angle.

My grandmother might be just pregnant with my mother but not know it yet. She's slight and shorter than Andrew, she's wearing a long dark dress. She's frowning and her hair is tied back but wisps fall forward onto her face.

'What about my father?' I say. It's a bald question but I don't know how else to ask.

'His name is Bob,' she says. 'He's a Catholic priest. I've never told anyone that before. I had to keep it a secret.' She smiles nervously and takes a long draw on her cigarette. 'I met him while I was at school. We became friends.' She sips her drink, someone opens the door, loud music floats over, we both look, it recedes. She looks back towards me, down at her cigarettes on the table. 'One night, we had too much to drink. We went to the beach for a walk. We had sex. Just the once.' She leans over. 'You know the worst thing? I hardly remember it. All I remember is that he kept repeating I can't stop now. He got sweaty and unkind. I wanted him to stop. He was so different. I was scared and dizzy from all the beer. And afterwards he said sorry he'd lost control and he had no right. Please don't cry he kept saying, this is hard enough. Please don't cry. But I couldn't stop crying. I sat there on the beach, my jeans down around my ankles, it was dark, I could hear and smell the sea and I couldn't stop crying. He walked me to the public toilets and told me to wash myself. He said a pregnancy was the last thing we needed.' She stops talking and I don't know what to say. Then she says, 'I didn't want to have sex with him. I wasn't even curious. No that's not true. I was curious.'

She was eighteen, Jane Kidman's age. She looks out to the

water. 'I couldn't tell anyone. I couldn't even tell my father. I had to tell them it was some fellow I met at a party. It took me a long time to forgive him for that. I still haven't really.'

'Did he think of leaving the priesthood and marrying you?'

'He did. I don't know. It was just wrong. I don't know if he'd want contact from you. I don't even know where he is.' I ask her why adoption. I try not to sound angry. 'Sometimes now when I look back on that time I wonder that I never gave a second thought to abortion. Anyone who found out I got pregnant said I was courageous. But I wasn't courageous. Abortion just wasn't an option for me. It wasn't something I thought about. Sometimes I wish I had.

'In the end, giving you up wasn't what I wanted. After you were there I mean, in the hospital. I just wanted to have you with me. It's hormonal I suppose. But I felt so alone.'

'Did you ever wonder what happened to me?'

'All the time, for years. But there wasn't anything I could do. I knew if I kept thinking of you, I'd go crazy. I had to get in control.' She stops, looks out at the water. 'Why did they call you Adele? Adele. What kind of a name is that? It's not the name I'd picked. I'd called you Lucinda, Lucinda Ferguson, after my father's mother. I thought they'd at least leave you with the name I gave you. But you see, that's what it's like, when you give someone up, you give all of them up. They could name you Simone or Carly or Cassandra and I'd have no control over it. Don't you see? If I didn't forget you, I'd be crazy. I don't expect you'd understand, I don't expect you'd have any idea what I'm talking about. It doesn't matter now. It just doesn't matter.' She looks out towards the water, her mouth set tight, her eyes opening and closing fast.

'I'm sorry I've brought all this up for you,' I say. 'I wanted to meet you and find out about who you are and who my father is.' I order us another drink. The sun is very bright. I get a sense of reality in bites, sitting at the beach, drinking white wine, with a perfect stranger who's my mother.

She agrees to a photograph. As she leaves she says, 'I'm sorry I haven't been better at this.' She looks away towards the sky. 'I wrote something back then,' she says. She takes out another envelope, drops it on the table. I sit quietly after she's gone, feel bashed about, as if I've struggled and come through an ordeal. I feel relaxed, not nervous, not angry, not sad. I feel my life in hard bites, I feel real.

Bill Pozzi was right. My adoption wasn't part of my father's framework, wasn't something he and my mother wanted to face, wasn't their responsibility, wasn't their story. And here was me, reminding them with each inch on the giraffe chart that one day I'd know the truth, growing more like myself and less like them every day, growing bigger and bigger. That's my story.

In the aeroplane, amid the comfort of low level noise, the kindness of flight attendants, my safe little seat with its buckle, I hold the envelope my mother gave me carefully in my two hands, wait for take-off, cruise flight, the first drink which comes with a little bowl of mixed nuts.

'Will you be dining this afternoon?' the flight attendant asks.

'Yes please,' I say.

There's a piece of paper in the envelope, folded twice, cream parchment, written over in a large loopy hand. I take my time unfolding it, let the moment pass. The flight attendant brings more wine with food. The man next to me tells me the fish is very good. Then I read, a poem of sorts.

When I saw you
the wrinkled dark pink
of your greasy skin
The fine black curls on your head
I
couldn't
imagine
we
shared my body
for so long.

You were the lump
the albatross.
You stopped me

drinking
smoking
living
finally living.
How could you
be born?

Your perfect fingers
nails
and eyes.
How did you come
from me?

Now you're gone
and
I ache
and ache
to see
you
again.

I drink more wine, look out to the sky, it's the blue of Greek window sills. I get an impression of something written on the wing, Jesus gin, but it couldn't be that. I try to keep my eyes open and look at the sun but I can't do it. I sit for a while, absently return my mother's poem to its envelope, seal it as best I can, place it in my bag, call for more wine.

# FORTY-EIGHT

When I arrive in Melbourne I go to a phone and call Bill Pozzi out of a meeting. 'Gareth Ford's guilty.'

He says he knows. 'Your secretary was worried about you. He brought the file up to my office.'

'What if I go to the press?'

'Daniel will sack you.'

'For breaching my new contract?'

'No doubt.' There's a flight announcement. 'What will you do?'

'I don't know Bill.'

'He's a liar,' Bill says.

'So's my father.'

I call my mother. 'I've been to see my birth mother,' I say. 'You should have told me years ago Mum. And so should Dad.' She says she knows, she's sorry. I say I didn't ring for apologies. 'I rang to say you should have told me and I forgive you.' I feel good when I hang up, better than I have in a long while. I ring Uncle Jack. I tell him where I've been. He says that's great, the R getting stuck in the back of his throat. I tell him I feel ready to see him again. He asks what she was like. 'She was like me,' I say. 'She thought she was scared of everything but she wasn't.' He doesn't say anything. 'Her family's Scottish,' I say. He says he knew it. 'She called me Lucinda.' He says it's a beautiful name. I tell him I love him. He doesn't say anything at first and then he says he loves me, too. I ring Emily, tell her to meet me at home, tell her I've got a long, long story to tell. She says it's about time.

Hilary isn't home when I get to Gareth's place and I'm relieved. When he answers the door, he looks frightened. It's funny, for so long I've seen him as much bigger than me, but today I feel as if he's shrunk. It's a beautiful day in Melbourne, the sun is out, it's warm, there's a soft breeze and more leaves on the elms since I went away this morning. I think I'd like a walk on the beach. Later.

We go to the lounge in the upstairs part of his house, he sits on the couch, I take a hard-back difficult chair. 'What can I say?' he says. He's holding his hand, rubbing one thumb into the other palm. I don't say anything. 'I'm sorry I lied to you. It wasn't something I wanted to do. If you want to punish me, I'll quit the university, I'll resign as a psychologist, I'll go into therapy, anything. I don't care anymore.' I don't say anything. I watch him. 'I'm willing to do just about anything. All I'm asking is one chance. Just one chance. Are you willing?'